1,000,000 Books

are available to read at

---◆---

www.ForgottenBooks.com

---◆---

Read online
Download PDF
Purchase in print

ISBN 978-1-331-10965-5
PIBN 10146048

This book is a reproduction of an important historical work. Forgotten Books uses
state-of-the-art technology to digitally reconstruct the work, preserving the original format
whilst repairing imperfections present in the aged copy. In rare cases, an imperfection in
the original, such as a blemish or missing page, may be replicated in our edition. We do,
however, repair the vast majority of imperfections successfully; any imperfections that
remain are intentionally left to preserve the state of such historical works.

Forgotten Books is a registered trademark of FB &c Ltd.
Copyright © 2018 FB &c Ltd.
FB &c Ltd, Dalton House, 60 Windsor Avenue, London, SW19 2RR.
Company number 08720141. Registered in England and Wales.

For support please visit www.forgottenbooks.com

1 MONTH OF
FREE
READING

at
www.ForgottenBooks.com

By purchasing this book you are eligible for one month membership to ForgottenBooks.com, giving you unlimited access to our entire collection of over 1,000,000 titles via our web site and mobile apps.

To claim your free month visit:
www.forgottenbooks.com/free146048

* Offer is valid for 45 days from date of purchase. Terms and conditions apply.

English
Français
Deutsche
Italiano
Español
Português

www.forgottenbooks.com

Mythology Photography **Fiction**
Fishing Christianity **Art** Cooking
Essays Buddhism Freemasonry
Medicine **Biology** Music **Ancient
Egypt** Evolution Carpentry Physics
Dance Geology **Mathematics** Fitness
Shakespeare **Folklore** Yoga Marketing
Confidence Immortality Biographies
Poetry **Psychology** Witchcraft
Electronics Chemistry History **Law**
Accounting **Philosophy** Anthropology
Alchemy Drama Quantum Mechanics
Atheism Sexual Health **Ancient History**
Entrepreneurship Languages Sport
Paleontology Needlework Islam
Metaphysics Investment Archaeology
Parenting Statistics Criminology
Motivational

THE

CHILD OF THE DESERT

BY

COL. THE HON. C. S. VEREKER

LIEUT.-COL. COMMANDANT, LIMERICK CITY ARTILLERY MILITIA

F.R.G.S.

AUTHOR OF "SCENES IN THE SUNNY SOUTH," ETC.

IN THREE VOLUMES

VOL. I.

LONDON

CHAPMAN AND HALL, 193, PICCADILLY

1878

[*All rights reserved*]

LONDON :

PRINTED BY VIRTUE AND CO., LIMITED,

CITY ROAD.

CONTENTS OF VOL. I

CHAPTER VI.

CHAPTER VII.

CHAPTER VIII.

CHAPTER IX.

CHAPTER X.

CHAPTER XI.

CHAPTER XII.

CHAPTER XIII.

CHAPTER XIV.

CHAPTER XV.

CHAPTER XVI.

THE CHILD OF THE DESERT.

CHAPTER I.

THE MARENGO GARDENS.

OUTSIDE the Bab-el-Oued Gate of Algiers, the Marengo Gardens cling to the side of the steep slopes that sweep down from the lofty towers of the Kasbah almost to the deep blue waters of the Mediterranean, laid out with the skilful taste of the landscape gardener, and adorned with rare flowers, trees, and shrubs.

Slender and graceful kiosks, erected in memory of holy Marabout saints, and bright with the rich though well-blended colours of the ena-melled encaustic tiles with which their sides are encrusted, stand in commanding sites, and form a grateful contrast to the tropical luxuriance of the spreading foliage, with its deep dense masses of verdure.

The far-spreading grounds rise up, terrace above terrace, as did of old the famed hanging

gardens of Babylon. Sheets of limpid water
intersect the gay parterres, while fountains of
pure white marble fling their cooling spray
upon the balmy air, and shady pools reflect the
beauties of the scene on their smooth surface,
unruffled save by the gold and silver fishes,
whose burnished sides unrestingly flash and
sparkle through the tide.

On one of the clear genial days of winter,
that bathe these southern shores in unfading
golden sunshine, the incongruous aggregation
of peoples and races that compose the population of the city thronged to the Jardin Marengo,
attracted by the music of a French military
band belonging to the garrison.

Ladies of Europe, whose toilettes bore evidence of the skill and taste of Parisian *modistes,*
mingled in the crowd with spectre-like figures of
veiled Arab and Moorish women, shrouded in
flowing white burnouses, their shuffling feet
pushed into unwieldy papouches; with Soudanese in caftans of dark-blue, striped with a
lighter shade of the same colour, their jet-black
yet benign and kindly faces calling to mind
the massive features of the Egyptian Sphinx;
and with sombre-clad Jewesses, having their
chins tied up in black silk kerchiefs, the least
becoming, ugliest style of head-dress ever invented by the most perverse ingenuity of female
vanity.

Attired in their haïks and burnouses, fat indolent Moors, blacks from the far South, scowling Arabs from the Tell and the Desert, Nomads
from the depths of the Sahara, M'zabites from
the Oases, and kindly-faced Kabyles from the
Djurjura and other ranges of the Atlas Mountains, brushed against the gay uniforms of their
conquerors; while chieftains of the native tribes,
together with Kadis, Marabouts, and Jews,
found themselves side by side with the European
colonists of the Sahel and the Metidja.

Such was the strangely assorted, heteroge-
neous crowd that promenaded round the kiosks
and parterres, or rested along the avenues of
bell-ombras, among whom Olinda Somerton
and her cousin Henry Wilton were sitting
beneath the shade of the evergreens and listening to the enlivening strains of the musicians.

Olinda loved music, and what the band was
playing pleased her much. It was a spirited
galop, somewhat differently arranged from
Arndt's *Eisenbahn* galop, and descriptive of the
journey by train from Blidah to Algiers across
the Metidja, charming by its freshness and
brilliancy; for, in addition to the imitation by
the instruments of the grating sound made by
the brake along the rails, the whistling and
screaming of the engine, and the rattle of the
moving train, the bandsmen reproduced in vocal
chorus the wild shouts and yellings of the excit-

able natives mounting and alighting at the various stations on the line, who raise a Babel-like din such as can scarce be realised by travellers accustomed to the orderly railways of Europe.

The sounds on a sudden became hushed, and the bandsmen murmured in subdued tones, when a gentleman close to Olinda informed her that a girl, stricken with the deadly palludian fever of Africa, was supposed to be assisted into the train at one of the stations, and that the spectators were expressing their condolence and their sympathy with the sufferer.

"Pretty, poetical idea," exclaimed Olinda, addressing her cousin, after thanking her neighbour, "but incapable, surely, of realisation, for a fever-stricken patient could scarcely be in a fit state to undertake a journey, or even to move from her sick-room."

"You are mistaken, Olinda," Wilton replied. "Last year, when travelling through the interior, I met several persons in various stages of this dreadful marsh-fever, some severely afflicted, but who were able, notwithstanding, to follow their daily avocations, though naturally under considerable difficulties. I remember, in particular, being driven in the province of Constantine by a diligence coachman who had barely sufficient strength to flog the jaded mules he was forcing along, so enfeebled was he by this terrible disease, as evinced by his quivering hands and chattering teeth. But, hark!" he continued, "we are coming to the grand *finale*."

The drums now beat, the trumpets loudly resounded, the cymbals clashed, and the voices of the bandsmen rose above all, copying the uproar and turmoil of the passengers as they struggled out of the carriages at the terminus in Algiers, and the shouts of the elbowing, shrieking crowd of Moorish, Jewish, French, Arab, and Kou'lourli porters and hotel touters let loose upon them, who furiously fought for their victims and clutched them in pitiless grasp, heedless of their loud remonstrances and bitter execrations.

This lively animated performance gave great delight to Olinda, who clapped her hands and joined heartily in the applause of the audience, as the sound of the thrilling strains rose aloft and awakened the echoes of the Kasbah above.

"Give me spirit-stirring music," she cried, "and not the tame insipid compositions one hears of late, which fail so signally to appeal to the feelings, or even to secure prolonged attention. We are told that a musical education is necessary before good music can be appreciated, or even understood; but I do not share this opinion. Music's mission, in my estimation, should be to appeal to and please the ear, in like manner as painting and sculpture appeal to and please the eye—a rule which artists and composers claiming to produce high-class works should carefully endeavour to follow. All those arts should adhere closely to Nature, portraying her as she appears under the most favourable and agreeable combinations, and rejecting everything barren of interest or unæsthetical. The painter and the sculptor would shrink from reproducing on canvas or in marble a bleak, flat, monotonous landscape, or a deformed ungainly specimen of the human race. Why then should the musician depart from this principle, and drench us with lifeless, soulless music?"

"You do not like high-class learned music then?" observed Wilton.

"On the contrary," she replied, "I entertain a very high respect for it, and I like it when heard in moderation."

"You mean, in fact, that a little goes a long way?" added Henry laughingly.

"Not exactly," she replied, "I do not quite mean that; for such a construction would seem to imply absence of all appreciation, and would so convey a false impression; the fact being that I do appreciate it, and own that it displays much merit and talent. But the spirit of the age is to run after this style to excess, like as the world, some years since, went crazy about the dry, crude, pre-Raphaelite school of painting. Both deserve all praise while kept within due bounds. Preserve me, though, from a gallery filled with only pre-Raphaelite pictures, or from a concert where long-winded, droning, noisy, unmelodious compositions alone are performed, the principal merit of which is that they are lengthy and so fill up the time. However, I must own that they are a lesser evil than the old variations on airs, invented with the purpose, apparently, of concealing the original melody under a dazzling cloud of runs, flourishes, and scales, for the greater glorification of the performer. In my humble estimation, the music of the future, notwithstanding its excellence and its high claims for praise, follows this pernicious example, consisting largely of difficult passages in the style of advanced exercises strung together for what I call mechanical manipulation, more than tasteful compositions calculated to please the ear through their harmonious cadences."

" Undoubtedly the first and chief aim of music should be to appeal through the ear to the feelings," Henry added.

"To the soul!" warmly interrupted Olinda. " That is talent."

"You are right," he replied, owning the justice of her correction. "Music that produces no deep emotion, no vivid impression, that has no palpable intelligible aim, I hold to be worthless —to be an unpardonable mistake."

"Listening to such is but waste of time," she added.

"Could an opera, for instance, succeed, or be even tolerated," Wilton went on, "that preserved throughout a uniform dead-level of mere unexciting instrumentation, however beautifully harmonized; that took but little heed of the vocal portion of the music, and that failed, in consequence, to depict the stirring scenes sought to be represented; that did not, in short, make the several characters engaged in the performance express themselves in tones of sorrow, joy, love, rage, despair, or pain, such as they were supposed to have experienced in real life, and such as the artists were delineating by their acting on the stage?"

"Undoubtedly it would be a gross departure from the eternal fitness of things," replied Olinda; "yet such have we seen, such have we suffered."

While thus conversing, a veiled Arab girl passed close in the crowd, accompanied by her black female attendant, whose tall, graceful, slender figure, as she glided by enveloped in her burnous, attracted Olinda's attention; and she pointed the girl out to Henry as far above the other native women in appearance, with their heavy ungainly figures and their shuffling underbred gait.

"Could that girl appreciate, and is she here

to admire, the music we have been listening to, I wonder?" observed Olinda, with a slight glance of derision; "or has she come from mere curiosity, to look on the animated scene and the gay dresses of the promenaders? Most probably from curiosity alone, for the poor degraded inmates of the harem vegetate in the grossest ignorance—beings whom it is hard to imagine gifted with musical tastes, or indeed with any mental refinement or accomplishment."

"Pardon me, Olinda, for contradicting you," Henry answered, " but many ladies of the harem devote much of their time to music."

"How do you know, pray?" asked Olinda, laughing.

" Only, of course, from what I hear secondhand," he answered, no little amused at the covert insinuation.

"Highly satisfactory explanation," she said in reply with mock gravity; "I feel perfectly satisfied."

"It must be owned, however," he continued, "that their music is but poor and worthless in character. It would require a severe course of preparation and education, I fancy, to make them even comprehend the dry heavy compositions we have just been discussing."

"Their knowledge of the Fine Arts must doubtless be very limited and superficial," added his cousin.

"Be that as it may," he went on, "I concur with you in thinking that girl has an appearance of superiority above the common herd of inanimate, soulless Mahometan women. She walks and carries herself with the air of a European—so different from those other creatures we see about us. Still they form no criterion to judge by, for the better class dare not in general venture to such a large concourse without the men of their family to guard them and watch their doings. Her appearance here, attended by only another young woman, is a mystery I cannot solve."

"No more can I," Olinda returned, "for she clearly belongs to a superior grade."

"She positively does seem a splendid creature, Olinda," he continued, still looking after the Arab; "and see! how her large lustrous black eyes flash above her yashmak! This system of veiling is a fatal blunder. Were she not covered up in that absurd manner, we could form a better estimate, and no doubt the inspection would prove highly satisfactory."

"I think so too," Olinda carelessly observed.

"That girl, somehow, has awakened a warm interest in me," he mused thoughtfully; "I wish we could look at the rest of her face."

"And that is not very likely to happen," she interposed.

"Well, it certainly is rather improbable," added Wilton in reply.

"But really the more one observes her," he began afresh, as he kept his eyes fixed on the Arab, "the stronger grows the conviction that she is fitted for better things than being shut up in a harem and consigned to a vapid existence of endless monotonous seclusion."

"The Bedouin seems to have made a serious impression on you, Henry," Olinda observed jestingly. "I believe you have fallen in love with her at first sight, in good old fairy-tale fashion."

"Pshaw! that would be too ridiculous," he interposed, annoyed at such a supposition. "Fancy my falling in love with one of those half-civilised creatures!" And he laughed scornfully at such a preposterous notion.

"As strange things have happened," said Olinda gaily.

"Speak not thus, Olinda, I entreat of you," he pleaded, for he was mortified at her suspecting him capable of such folly. "It pains me that you think so poorly of my sense."

"Do not take up my thoughtless words so seriously," said the kind-hearted girl. "Why should you not copy King Cophetua, if you like?"

"Or Peter the Great?" he added, striving to conceal his vexation at her affront to his understanding. "You know the famous Empress Catherine, whom he married, was a young Livonian orphan girl, brought up in the house of a Lutheran minister, and so obscure in her origin that she was known only by the name of 'Martha.' She first married a sergeant in the Swedish army, who was shortly afterwards killed in battle by the Russians. General Bauer, the Russian commander, seeing her after the battle, took her under his protection, and placed her in charge of his establishment. Subsequently she remained under the protection of Prince Menchikoff, who had formerly been a scullion in the Czar's service, until, at the early age of seventeen, she captivated the Czar by her beauty and great talents, and exchanged the mansion of the prince for the palace of the sovereign, being crowned Empress, some years after, with great pomp and magnificence. So you see that, with such a precedent, there is nothing so very absurd after all in admiring that shrouded houri."

Then she gave him one of her sweet winning smiles, that chased away his momentary annoyance.

"But, look!" he went on, seeing the Arab cast back a last, long, lingering glance as she turned from them, after his eyes and hers had met; "she perceives we are speaking of her, and is moving away."

The girl did indeed observe Wilton's gaze, and the intuitive knowledge that he was admiring her, and praising her to his companion, sent her hot African blood coursing swiftly through her swelling veins.

Olinda and Wilton little suspected the instantaneous havoc wrought in Azzahra's fiery nature by those fleeting looks interchanged, heedless though they were upon Wilton's part, nor the influence they were destined to produce hereafter.

Notwithstanding the warm encomiums Wilton passed on the Arab, he thought but lightly as yet of her proud commanding figure, of her flashing eye, of her graceful walk, and of the refinement with which her manner was stamped. His desire to see the haïk dropped, so that he might regard the fresh young features it concealed, was prompted by curiosity alone. As to love, the thought never once crossed his mind ; he would have despised himself for such imbecility.

He admired none, cared for none, asked for none, save his fair gifted cousin beside him, whom he counted the most lovely and the most perfect of women, as he drank in the beauty of her deep blue eye, of her rich flowing golden hair, of her lithe and slender figure, and of the sweet gentle expression that gleamed from her delicately chiselled features.

And Olinda fully merited his warmest admiration and love. In her bright beaming countenance were vividly reflected her virtuous mind, her sweet disposition, her lofty intellect, and her noble soul—qualities which, joined to the sweet benign smile that ever played about her lips, secured universal homage and esteem.

Yet had she two faults, and grievous faults, fatal to her happiness; for they reared up an insurmountable barrier between herself and her young cousin, whose intense passion for her she would otherwise have doubtless returned.

Unfortunately for herself, she was afflicted with an unceasing, ever-present conviction of her own intellectual superiority to those around, and likewise with a morbid weakness for running after and worshipping "talent" in others. She could never refrain from remembering that she was gifted with abilities of no ordinary character; while Wilton, it was idle to deny to herself, was not thus blessed. The consequence was that she looked down upon him, though with a gentle, kindly, sorrowful feeling of regret, as her mental inferior, at the same time liking him greatly, loving him even in a cousinly way, and taking sincere pleasure in his society. She often sighed, she knew not why, when she thought of the separating chasm, and of how different might have been their lot had Fate otherwise decreed. Still there yawned the chasm, and she saw no way of bridging it over.

Their lives were so different!

The occupations she loved were study and the cultivation of her taste for the Fine Arts. The pursuit of art was indeed her ruling passion, and in art she excelled, for she could do all things well—too well for her own happiness, because her proficiency, and the consequent power it gave, produced a reprehensible feeling of vain false pride that ill accorded with her gentle nature.

Wilton, on the other hand, was devoted, with the manly instincts of youth, to outdoor pursuits and to society; troubling himself little, as she imagined, about mental culture.

But she was mistaken.

Following up the advantages of the liberal education he had received, he always kept *au courant* with the literature and topics of the day, although, through mortified pride, making no attempt before her to display his acquirements.

This Olinda would have discovered had she taken the pains to study his character; but, carried away by perverse self-sufficiency, she neglected to adopt this simple method of weighing him in the balance, and of bringing to light his noble qualities and his great inherent worth, so certain of development hereafter when the frivolities of youth had passed.

Thus it came to pass that she wrecked the happiness which might have been hers.

In all external refined accomplishments Henry was unquestionably her inferior, thanks to the misguided system of education in our schools and colleges; yet he was not so much her inferior in intellectual capacity, nor even in information on general subjects, as she chose to believe.

Still, no doubt, a wide gulf of dissimilarity did separate them, for what sympathy could exist between persons of such widely divergent tastes? And, in truth, their characters were equally divergent.

He was of an impulsive loving temperament, good-natured, and easily led; but he lacked, owing to youth, that decision of purpose and firmness of will which woman loves to honour in him she would look upon as her future lord.

She, on the other hand, was somewhat cold and imperious. Conscious in her strength, she had the misfortune to exhibit, though unintentionally and without a tinge of arrogant assumption, that tone of priority which man, in spite of himself, cannot refrain from resenting in woman.

This feeling, although unknown to himself, he had begun to experience and nurture. He did often resent the ungentle, authoritative tone she assumed, and the manner in which she asserted a more elevated position than himself.

She could estimate the dissimilarity and the divergence. She could perceive the transparent difficulties and obstacles in their path, created by their uncongenial nature and habits. But from him all this was hidden, by reason of his unreasoning devotion. He believed that, were she once his bride, the bright feminine side of her character would assert its sway, leading her to renounce her deplorable vanity, and her still more deplorable passion for talent-worship, that threatened to become the bane of her future life. He believed she would turn her thoughts instead to the enjoyment of home, to the discharge of her conjugal duties, and to devotedness towards her husband. Of her innate goodness of heart and sweetness of disposition he never entertained a doubt. So he continued to dwell in hope.

Olinda formed a different and a juster estimate of herself. She judged that, however contentedly and happily she might live with a kindred spirit—with a man she could look up to and honour—she would not be justified, for her cousin's sake as well as her own, in allying herself with a husband whom she could not regard as a superior, or at least as an equal.

And she judged aright.

To her handsome cousin she would have gladly surrendered her hand did she think she could have given her heart as well; for she honoured his open manly nature and his many estimable qualities. More than she was aware of, too, she admired his noble prepossessing person, his well-moulded features, and his fascinating manners.

But overweening vanity stood in the way, blinding and perverting her judgment.

Yet was not hers altogether a purely egotistical form of vanity. Her high self-estimate did not smother better and more exalted feelings. She desired not, like too many of her sex when they learn their power, to obtain the mastery over her future lord, and to make his will subservient to hers. On the contrary, she sighed for one, should Fate compel her to give up her liberty, to whom she might tender entire unconditional submission—on whom she might pour out her pure unselfish love. Of him she would be vain, she thought—vainer far than she felt of herself now. Such only should be her lord and master; with such only could she live contented; to such only could she be loving and dutiful.

To this exaggerated ideal standard Henry, with all his merits, undoubtedly failed to attain; wherefore she gently repulsed him whenever he approached the subject of love, as she felt that honour and affectionate regard for him demanded, since their union—feeling towards him as she did—seemed impossible.

Had her thoughts been less concentrated on her talents, she would have seized with thankfulness such an opportunity to seal her happiness, instead of idly indulging in remote visionary speculations—never in all probability to be realised.

But she could not distinguish nor value the boon within her reach. She shrank from abandoning her cherished pursuits and amusements to embark on an unknown sea, and to be drawn into the vortex of a new life. She cared not to surrender her independence and her freedom for what seemed of very doubtful advantage.

Most of her sex would have rejoiced to secure such a husband as Wilton — would have felt grateful for being rescued from the hated shoals and quicksands of single-blessedness.

Few men indeed of any fortune or position are to be met, even though not up to the standard of personal attraction, who cannot find plenty of the opposite sex eager to accept their proposals, sooner than incur the dreaded risk of remaining "spinneys" for the rest of their days.

But sordid and interested motives, that occupy the minds of the fair—instilled, alas! in many cases under the instruction of scheming, manœuvring, heartless mothers — found no place in Olinda's lofty soul. Their mercenary daydreams were unknown, unthought of; or, if

thought of, were dismissed with scorn, as beneath the notice of a virtuous honourable
woman. For her the prospect of brilliant con-
nection, high position, the pleasures of dissipation, boundless wealth, jewels, slaves at her
feet, jealous rivals, adoring admirers, possessed
no attractions.

Such adventitious, evanescent enjoyments she
needed not to secure happiness. Perfect contentment was hers, alone in her secluded boudoir,
studying her favourite authors, playing her
favourite melodies, singing her favourite songs,
working up the sketches she had taken out-of-
doors of her favourite haunts. No more she
sighed for, save the friendship and love of those
around her. With them she gladly mingled in
social intercourse, though she coldly shrank
from plunging into the vortex of the great world
—into what she would always term " scenes of
frivolity and dissipation," scenes so eagerly
sought by girls of her own age and position.

This ungenial and misanthropical turn of
mind was a fatal error, engendered by the over-
strained religious teaching and narrow-minded
bigotry of a silly puritanical mother—an error
so prolific of future danger, so likely to drive
the recluse into the opposite extreme on dis-
covering that it is an error.

She had recently overcome these homely prejudices to attend a brilliant ball given by the

Governor-General of Algeria in his beautiful Moorish palace. But curiosity rather than the love of pleasure had been the attraction. For her the regal splendour of that glittering scene possessed no charms of fascination; to her it gave no pleasure. Joining not in the amusements and gaiety of the smiling throng, she sighed for the hour when she could leave what she regarded as the senseless levity and the flimsily disguised depravity she beheld on every side, to seek again the peace and quiet of her home. She sighed for rational sensible conversation— a plant that, of a surety, thrives but seldom in the atmosphere of the ballroom.

Poor, vain, weak, misguided woman! to set up such an exaggerated, such an unattainable ideal! Wait till the end comes; then how will you judge your own conduct? Will you not regret your unwisdom? Will you not mourn and weep over the past?

Preachers, who from your pulpits unwittingly advocate impossibilities by urging a life of morose ungenial seclusion, do you ever pause to reflect what harm you do in hardening the hearts of your hearers, and driving them into hostility through your bigotry and intolerance? Do you ever reflect that they ought not to adopt the course you recommend? Do you reflect that should they, in a moment of weakness, follow your pedantic ill-judged advice, turning their backs on their friends, and abandoning that state of life in which they have been placed, their social position will sooner or later force them to relinquish such unwise, such unnatural misanthropy, will force them back into what you call "the world"? Then will not the last state be worse than the first?

Wilton noticed throughout the evening, with profound sorrow, this shrinking, gloomy, puritanical spirit, for to him these *réunions*, with their gay lightheartedness, brought unmingled pleasure; and he employed every device, but unsuccessfully, to make his fair cousin share his enjoyment.

His regret went further than solicitude for Olinda. He thought of Geraldine as well, his favourite sister. She had been adopted by her aunt, Alice Thornton, with whom she and Olinda were on a visit during their stay at Algiers; and he thought of the *triste* existence the child would lead should Olinda, during his absence, acquire influence over her sufficient to rear her up with these morose ideas. He desired to see the girl mingle and associate with her equals, not to live shut out from the world in which, by birth and position, she was entitled to move.

But he need have felt no such anxiety. Geraldine's sympathies and predilections all tended the opposite way. She was a bright, sunny, happy child, whom his mother at her death had left in his charge. Although a con- firmed little coquette, precocious and *prononcée* far beyond her years, and full of mischievous frolic, she was, nevertheless, thoroughly amiable and good at heart.

Devotion to her exercised a strong influence over Wilton. It gave an additional impulse to urge his suit for Olinda's hand, for, were Olinda his wife, he would always be near to look after and watch the child, and save her young life from becoming spoiled and soured through being righteous overmuch. He could then find means as well to modify Olinda's extreme views, which, after all, were an error on the right side.

As to Geraldine becoming righteous over- much, never was apprehension less called for; no blighting influence could scathe her—she lived within a fairy circle of perpetual joy and sunshine.

"I have had immense fun, Henry," ejaculated Geraldine, in her lively impulsive manner, as she ran up to Wilton. "You have actually made a conquest of one of those horrible ghosts that look so dreadful stalking about in their white shrouds. Fancy, I heard her tell that hideous black girl with her that you were the handsomest man she had ever seen."

"Nonsense, you little naughty puss! What

folly you talk!" Henry replied, pretending to
give her a slap on the cheek.

"It is true, though," Geraldine continued
with the merry pertness of childhood; "and,
what is more, she went on to say she could see
you were as deeply smitten with her as she
was with you, for you never took your eyes off
her."

Wilton laughed heartily at what Geraldine
told, yet did it flatter him at heart. Who is
proof against the incense of flattery?

"This is a nice scrape you have got me into,
Olinda," exclaimed Henry, turning to his cousin,
and merrily laughing. "It was very wrong to
make me look after the poor girl until she
fancied I was love-smitten. But for you, I should
never have noticed her in the crowd."

"If I never get you into a worse scrape than
that," returned Olinda gaily, "you may esteem
yourself highly fortunate."

"Indeed, I think so," Henry carelessly answered.

And they rose to depart after having been
joined by Miss Thornton, whose admiring contemplation of the selection of music played by
the band had been cruelly interfered with by the
manner in which, as she declared, a little round
fat French colonel, with a bullet-shaped head,
closely-cropped hair, and a red fierce face,
gazed on her so as to cover her with blushing

confusion. Poor simple creature! she firmly believed the gallant Gaul was eying her in silent admiration of her charms, whereas he was surveying that antique and strangely attired lady as an interesting yet forbidding specimen of the strange sojourners in *perfide Albion!*

CHAPTER II.

WHEN the band ceased the large assemblage rapidly dispersed, some to descend through the gardens and so re-enter the city by the Gate Bab-el-Oued; others to mount along the wide road that winds up in zigzags past the Kasbah, or Palace of the Deys under the rule of the Turks.

The latter route our party followed. Pursuing the route El-Biar, that runs outside the dense Arab quarter of the town, but inside the powerful French lines of earthwork circumvallation, Henry and Olinda came to where it passes along the ancient Moorish walls of the city. These walls are composed of immense blocks of chinarro—clay baked into a solid red mass of brickwork by mere exposure, while in a moistened state, to the scorching sunbeams of an African summer.

"How like the glorious old walls of the Alhambra!" exclaimed Olinda, calling to mind the happy days they had all passed in Granada.

" Just the same colours as those lovely vermilion towers I loved so well to sketch."

Wilton and his cousin walked on for some time in silence, musing on the past—she with pleasure, he with sadness.

" I hope to revisit those delightful scenes some day," she at length resumed. " Well might the Emperor Charles exclaim, referring to the expulsion by his grandfather of Boabdil the Unlucky, ' Unhappy the man who lost such a terrestrial paradise !' "

This allusion to their sojourn in the Land of the Moor brought back painful recollections to Wilton's mind. He had long been deeply enamoured of his fair cousin, and, until their visit to Granada, he always cherished the hope that she would learn by degrees to reciprocate his affection. But he suspected that his difficulty lay in the fact that Olinda experienced not the anxiety and ambition felt by most women to enter the married state—indeed that, on the contrary, she shrank from such a change of life. He discovered the certainty of this at Granada, where more than once he sounded her feelings, and found, to his disappointment, that the subject of love she ever studiously avoided, checking on every occasion, with gentle firmness, the slightest declaration of admiration or affection.

On this account, although in her society day by day, he had long abstained from all such attempts to win her, deeming it more prudent to wait than to press his suit against her inclination. While he maintained unbroken silence, however, on the subject so dear to his thoughts, his mind would often recur to his former hopes. He trusted that constant daily intercourse, and Time, the great rectifier of human ills, would gradually and imperceptibly soften her heart, so effecting his purpose—slowly, it might be, but still surely.

Ofttimes, when pondering over his bitter disappointment, and reflecting how seldom the course of true love runs smoothly, he remembered with pain the days—so happy while gliding past, so sad to look back on—that they had spent together in the Land of the Moor. To-day all came back afresh to his mind. He remembered the scene beneath the sculptured colonnades of the Generalife Palace, after they had long stood gazing down together at the wondrously beautiful prospect below their feet, where the glowing red towers of the Alhambra, the quaint old Moorish city of Granada, the fertile Vega still irrigated as it was left by the industrious Moors, and the lofty snow-clad ranges of the Sierra Nevada, all lay stretched out before them in one vast glorious panorama.

He remembered how they walked together through the beautiful court of the palace, gay with choicest flowers, along the margin of the rapid, sparkling, icy torrent that glides beneath its bowers of roses, and past the huge towering old cypress-trees, within one of whose trunks, hollowed out by age, tradition relates that Zorayah, the beautiful Christian Sultana, concealed herself when in fear of being discovered with her lover by the Moorish monarch.

He remembered how Olinda maintained that the outraged Sultan was justified in hewing the traitress to pieces on the spot with his scimitar, when he had dragged her forth from her hiding-place, arguing that woman deserves no mercy who wantonly betrays her trust—who wrongs the man she has solemnly sworn to honour and obey.

He remembered how he had prized Olinda for giving utterance to such virtuous indignation, though unable at the time to suppress a smile at the manner in which her enthusiasm carried her away to take so lenient a view of despotic retributive justice, and what trusting confidence she inspired in his breast as to her truthfulness and purity.

He remembered how he had gazed in her eyes, as he softly whispered what happiness she could confer were he able to win her heart; and how she had turned her head away, making some cold repellent reply, as though she seemed to hear and heed him not.

All this he remembered, for unconsciously she

had touched the keynote, rousing afresh the passion he had so long striven to repress, by referring to those bygone days.

She was more lovely than ever, he thought. A rich warm glow suffused her cheeks, a sweet smile lighted up her face; she was radiant with life and spirits, bright and happy.

They were alone, and he determined, on the impulse of the moment, to make one more attempt to gain her.

"You cannot but know well, Olinda," he began, looking fondly into her soft expressive eyes with the fervid ardour of youth, " the great love I bear you, although ever since you showed me such marked coldness at Granada I have studiously kept silence. But it is impossible you can remain unconscious that my devotion is as deep and unalterable as ever. Why, save to be near you, should I thus follow in your footsteps? Why seek each scene you seek? Why constitute myself your devoted slave, ready to gratify your slightest wish? You think perhaps I am here for the sake of my sister. That is a strong inducement I grant, but not sufficient. It is for your sake, Olinda, I come, and for yours alone."

Then Olinda replied in freezing, forbidding tones, for she had not yet learned the great mystery of love, nor could she comprehend its wild, intoxicating, maddening power over the human heart. "You truly believe your love for me is deep and lasting, Henry, I feel convinced, or you would scorn to speak thus; but what proof have you that you read your own mind aright?—that yours is not a fleeting, evanescent caprice, fickle as the breeze that blows upon the mountain-side? Love is very false, very deceptive; he delights to blind our eyes and to stultify our understandings."

"Then he has failed to blind or stultify me," Henry retorted. "On the contrary, he has opened my eyes, so that I can see aright. I swear to you, Olinda, by all I hold dear and sacred, that I love you each day with a deeper and more devoted love!"

"But cannot you perceive, Henry, that although I like you as my cousin, and enjoy your society," replied Olinda, stricken with insensate blindness, "our tastes and pursuits are too widely dissimilar for us to think of marriage? You are devoted, like most men of your age and station in life, to the sports of the field, to society, and to the excitement of active life. My predilections are in the opposite direction. I never feel so contented as when alone in retirement, with my music, my painting, and my books, shut off from the whirl and turmoil of the great, hollow, deceptive, depraved outer world. Why then should two such unkindred spirits seek to be bound and chained together? Is it not far, far wiser that we each should follow our respective ways? Why should I make myself a martyr by joining in your festive scenes? Why should you become a victim by abjuring social intercourse, and restricting yourself, for my sake, to unappreciated home occupations? Such a course would not be wise. Believe me, it would not. Besides, remember the happy terms of intimacy we meet on now, both free, and un-fettered by indissoluble ties. How different would it be, think you, after marriage, with each bound to consult the wishes and caprices of the other? Be advised then, Henry, and relinquish for ever this imprudent infatuation. Did you succeed, you would inevitably repent of your choice."

"Never, I swear!" he interrupted with wild energy.

"Yes, you would," she quietly pursued, un-heeding his passionate expostulations. "When you marry, you must choose some merry light-hearted girl, fond, like yourself, of conviviality and amusement; and if perforce I ever change my condition—a change I desire not—I will endeavour to become the wife of a man with tastes and thoughts and habits congenial to my own. Indeed, indeed, you would not secure your happiness united to me, much as I should strive conscientiously to fulfil my duty, did I once consent to our union. Besides, with your ardent temperament, you are still too young in mind, though not in years, for settling down to the dull routine of domestic existence. A man with such a nature cannot commit a graver blunder than to give up his liberty too early in life. If you follow my advice, you will not think of marriage for years to come, and I pride myself in having some little knowledge of human nature."

"But you would guide me and reform me, Olinda," he humbly but ardently interrupted. "I should look up to you as my good angel, to whom I should soon learn to devote my whole existence."

"For a time perhaps life would thus fleet past pleasantly enough," she sorrowfully answered, "but by-and-by the end would come. You would begin to pine for your merry companions, for your accustomed amusements, for your scenes of gaiety and even, it may be, of dissipation. You would soon become wearied of me and my homely habits."

"Olinda, for Heaven's sake," he exclaimed in a voice of despair, "break not my heart by such terrible accusations and such melancholy forebodings!—by such dread prophecies of ill! Surely you cannot comprehend the depth of my love, or you would spare me this cruel torture!"

"Ah! what I say is too true," Olinda

answered. "Believe my words, your alliance with me would not be conducive to our mutual happiness; on that point I am fully assured. Yet, without happiness, of what avail is life? Is it not a dreary waste, an empty void? Fly such a doom, Henry! Fly it, as you value your fate in this world, or in the world to come!"

"Alas! alas! there may be truth and justice, after all, in the view you take," he sorrowfully answered, after pondering for some moments, carried away for the time, and humbled in his own estimation by her cold calculating arguments. "Perhaps I am unworthy to possess so priceless a treasure. Priceless indeed you are, for where can a woman be found with so noble a soul as yours? But, oh! have patience, Olinda," he continued, resuming his impassioned appeal, after a pause of wavering hesitation. "Have patience, and you can mould me to your will; you can raise me to your own level; you can render me worthy of you. You can make me the happiest and the most blessed of men."

"Ah! I disbelieve in these sudden transformations," she said, with a sigh. "Man invariably follows the instincts of his youth. Vain is the effort to withstand the all-powerful influences they exert; for, believe me, no harder task exists than to reform and eradicate deeply rooted customs and prejudices. In childhood the character may be changed and moulded at will, but never thoroughly in after years. Embark not in such a wild crusade—in such a hopeless conflict with Nature. You will shipwreck yourself in the attempt."

Henry could not but feel the force of what she said.

"Beyond doubt, when one comes to man's estate," he assented, his faith in himself shaken afresh, "the character is unalterably formed, whether for good or evil. I should fare but ill, I know, in striving to alter mine, or to master the accomplishments in which you shine, so as to reach your standard. The man who wins you must of a surety be of no ordinary stamp. Each day you command more and more my admiration and esteem. Each day I own more helplessly how far you rise above me. Unhappily for my peace of mind, my self-respect decreases in the inverse ratio according as my appreciation of you increases. In the same proportion as I honour you, I despise myself for being so far beneath your level. Thus have I become the most wretched of men. Would that in early days I had been taught all you know, instead of wasting my years, at the beck of obstinate, narrow-minded, pedantic preceptors and professors, on the study of obsolete languages that have never been of advantage to me since, and that never can be of advantage to me in after-life! Had I been fitted, as you are, to take my part in the great intellectual, cultivated world, how differently would you have thought of me! —how differently would you have felt towards me! How happy we two should have been together, imbued with the same tastes, wrapped up in the same pursuits! But it is idle to look back on the past, which can never be recalled."

"You must not speak thus, my dear Henry," she hastily yet tenderly interrupted, "or you will break up our happy family circle by forcing me to leave. How could I conscientiously or honourably remain here, to behold you overwhelmed with sorrow, the unhappy victim of a hopeless · passion, which separation from me would cure? It is but natural and right that you should stay, for the sake of the sister of whom you are so fond. If you fail, therefore, to overcome this fleeting fancy, I must surely take my departure."

"Would it were but a fleeting fancy!" he sighed. "It is a deep burning love, Olinda, which death alone can extinguish."

"You judge wrongly, Henry—indeed you do!" Olinda replied in saddened accents. "Your love is no more than a fleeting fancy, mark my words. My instincts tell me this with unmistakable distinctness. Oh, may it prove a true conviction! May you speedily emancipate yourself from this thraldom! for my heart would break to know you stricken down, through me, with mental suffering. I love you too much—as my cousin, I mean—to make you grieve without hope after one who, after all, may be unworthy of your manly, generous, chivalrous nature. Shake off the galling shackles of this boyish weakness; do it for my sake, Henry, I implore of you! What happy companions we may then be together again, instead of regarding each other with suspicious and distant reserve!"

For some moments Wilton's heart was too full to speak.

"Is this your final resolve, Olinda?" he at length demanded, as he gave her an imploring look, after long communing with himself in silence.

"Yes, Henry, it is," was the reply. "May God, in His mercy, bless you, and guide you aright, my dear cousin! Oh, how I pray that I may be acting for the best!—that the future of both may be influenced for good by my decision to-day! How I pray that one may fall to my lot, should I ever change my condition, as good, as honourable as you!"

"After such a declaration," Wilton answered, his voice almost choked with the intensity of his emotion, "I pledge myself, Olinda, to conform to your wishes by not reopening the subject again—unless indeed you give me permission, or at least until you show by your altered demeanour that my addresses are no longer unacceptable."

"You have done well to form this resolve," Olinda kindly murmured in response. "Your feelings, believe me, are not so strong, not so deep, as you imagine ; only a manly effort is required to burst the chain and get free. Some day, perhaps not so far distant, you will find to your astonishment that my estimate was correct, and that I read your character aright. Then will you thank me for having opened your eyes so as to make you know yourself—the great problem for the study of mankind, a problem so few of us, alas ! know how to solve."

He smiled incredulously at her prophecies, but made no reply, as they walked on together in silence within the precincts of the Kasbah— strangers yet—so near, and yet so far.

How amazed he would have been did he know with what accuracy of judgment Olinda had summed up his character, had gauged and measured his love !

She was right in her opinion that, although so amiable and so gentle, he was possessed of too proud a spirit to content himself with the second place, his inevitable position if married to her, and that after a time he would begin to chafe, though probably in secret, under the intolerable yoke. She was right in thinking that a woman of less ambitious temperament, of

less elevated mental calibre, and of a more social
genial nature than hers, would be better fitted to
become his wife. She was right in believing
the wound she had inflicted might soon be
healed, and its existence forgotten. She was
right in refusing him her hand—at least for the
present.

But to Henry the future was a sealed book.
The events of the passing moment and the
mental misery he endured were solely engrossing his thoughts. Yet, though his heart was so
full of grief, he made a manly effort to master
his feelings, and he succeeded.

They were now close to the Kasbah.

The black, yawning, cavern-like mouth of the
entrance to the fortress was before them, with its
massive iron grating, from which, in olden times,
few of the victims ever came out alive who were
imprisoned within by the despotic Viceroys of
the Porte.

They stopped to look at these relics of the
past, and to think of the dark deeds of blood
and the foul crimes committed within those
dismal dungeons during the Moslem rule, under
the sacred name of Justice.

Wilton feigned an interest he felt not, for he
wished to make believe he was putting away his
sorrow and wearing the willow no more.

He was telling Olinda how one of the Deys
had massacred in cold blood for rebellion the

whole of the Kou'lourlis, or sons of the Turks
by native women, when Alice Thornton and
Geraldine overtook them. On Miss Thornton
hearing that the greater number of these unhappy men had been blown away from the guns
on the walls, and that the remainder had been
hacked to pieces with scimitars, and their
mangled remains flung into the sea, her sensi-
tive nature was so deeply outraged that she
commenced to bewail their tragic fate, and to
pour forth exclamations of horror at such relent-
less bloodshed.

This outburst of sentimentalism gave great
amusement to Geraldine, who loved to see her
aunt puzzled, or shocked, or frightened.

She asked the old lady, with her merry ring-
ing laugh, whether she had ever heard of the
famous Chiaoux who beheaded such a number
of men.

"No? Then I will tell you," the child went on,
highly entertained by Miss Thornton's horrified
expression. "This terrible Turk in one day
struck off with his own hand the heads of no
less than a hundred and thirty-four Arab de-
serters from the army of the Viceroy, setting
them up afterwards in a row upon the spikes
that surmounted the Gate Bab-Azzoun. Now
confess, Aunt Alice, would you not like to have
seen this wholesale executioner?"

"The abominable wretch!" screamed out

Miss Thornton; "I would not look on such a monster for all the world."

Affecting astonishment at such want of curiosity, Geraldine, with a mischievous twinkle in her eye, declared it must have been highly interesting to hear this remarkable man describe the minutiæ of his wonderful performance.

"Highly interesting? Horribly revolting, you mean!" her aunt replied, with a shudder.

And another merry peal came from Geraldine's light heart.

These harmless sallies Olinda always discouraged. She considered it highly reprehensible for a young child thus to mock her seniors and turn them into ridicule, although done through mere good-natured frivolity.

She gave her young cousin a look of reproof, and, changing the conversation, remarked what a boon had been conferred on civilisation by expelling the Turkish Deys from the Kasbah, and overthrowing their blood-stained, tyrannical despotism.

"The French make only indifferent colonists," she continued, "but they have at least introduced a righteous system of government, for which they deserve the gratitude of Christendom."

"Yes, in this way they atone for the outrage they committed in seizing on these territories," Wilton replied. "It was an unjustifiable breach of faith with the other nations of Europe."

"But what would you have had done?" she continued. "The Algerine corsairs were a pest and a constant danger throughout the entire Mediterranean, and their extinction had become an imperative necessity. Far from endeavouring to stamp out piracy, the Turkish Viceroys fostered and pampered these outlaws, abhorred of all the world, for the sake of the wealth—the plunder and slaves—they gained for the country by their lawless depredations. Did not Justice then loudly demand that such a system of rule should be destroyed?"

"No form of administration, I admit, could be more degraded," replied Wilton, "than that which flourished in the Kasbah under the sway of the Turks."

"And does not the same system of misrule prevail to this day in all the Turkish provinces both of Europe and Asia?" she pursued.

"Too true," Henry answered. "Nowhere can there be found security for life or property. But let us hope that a better form of administration is about to be introduced."

CHAPTER III.

THE KASBAH.

WHILE they were thus conversing outside the gateway, a dashing young French officer of Hussars came out of the Kasbah, clattering his sword along the pavement as he walked in the bravura manner so dear to his compatriots. Politely accosting the party, he offered his services to conduct them through the old Palace, now completely metamorphosed and converted into barracks—an offer gladly accepted.

In appearance he was highly prepossessing. Tall and slight, with delicately chiselled features, his bright searching black eyes and his firmly set mouth proclaimed him to possess marked decision of character and commanding intellectual power.

Offering his arm to Olinda, and expressing regret at the interior of the Kasbah having been so changed through demolitions and alterations that the original plan of the old structures could scarcely be traced, he led the way within, conversing with the air and manners of a citizen of the world.

He had not gone far before he commenced to bewail his cruel fate at suffering exile in a remote corner of the earth, far removed from his beloved Paris, where his brightest visions and aspirations were concentrated.

This confession should have opened Olinda's eyes to his true character. She should have discovered that he resembled the great bulk of the *jeunesse dorée* of his country, in sighing after the excitements and the dissipation of the capital, and in abjuring the dull monotony of an uneventful secluded existence. Instead of tracing his impatience of expatriation to its true cause, she got carried away with the delusion that he pined only for a larger field wherein to develop the brilliant intellectual powers she could plainly perceive he possessed.

Under his guidance they entered the great central court.

This court, though now an ordinary barrack-square, in the time of the Deys was paved with white marble, and was surrounded above, as are all Moorish houses, by a gallery which gave access to all the upper chambers of the palace. This gallery surmounted a long range of clois-tered colonnades, and rested on columns of pure white marble.

The Marquis de St. Bertrand (for such was

the title of the gallant French officer) conducted them up into this gallery, to show the spot where the daïs of the Dey had stood at the farther end, over which a crimson carpet was spread for him to sit upon, while he held his divan to give audience to foreign envoys and other strangers of distinction.

Geraldine thought how lovely this gallery must have looked, decorated throughout its entire length with mirrors, cabinets, rich caskets, and a profuse collection of articles of luxury and objects of art, so as to call to mind, amid such a dazzling blaze of light, the great Hall of Mirrors at Versailles.

The child bewailed to her aunt the departure of all this glory and beauty, so that the place thereof knew it no more. She regretted above all the loss of the mirrors, at which they could have stopped to survey their charms if still hanging up on the walls.

"You know, Aunt Alice, you would have liked to admire your dear old face," the child rattled on, putting her arm caressingly round Miss Thornton. "How delightful to have lived here of old! I should have enjoyed it beyond measure, and so would you, I know very well!"

This sally St. Bertrand overheard, and he was highly entertained by the child's precocious remarks, which he could perceive were intended to make fun of her aunt; for when his eye fell on

Miss Thornton's laughable figure, he saw how little cause existed in her case for admiration in a looking-glass—a conclusion, however, that good lady herself was far from sharing.

Descending by a staircase to the bottom of this gallery, their guide pointed out where stood formerly the door of the subterranean treasury, protected by massive locks and by a strong wicket-gate.

"Inside this door," observed Raoul de St. Bertrand, "extended a long corridor with extensive caves branching off right and left, into which no light nor air could penetrate, and which were divided by massive partitions of stone. In these gloomy chambers glittering heaps were strewn of gold and silver money of all ages and all countries, together with the rarest jewels and precious stones."

"What a gorgeous sight!" exclaimed Geraldine in wonder. "Would that all these treasures were piled up below yet, and that I might run down and have a little quiet pilfering! A few diamonds and rubies would never be missed from such a mass of gems. But do tell me, Monsieur St. Bertrand," she went on, as they entered the court again, "whereabouts was the harem situated? I must see the harem, where so many beautiful creatures were collected together, and where they passed such happy lives, surrounded by every luxury and enjoyment, with no troubles, no cares—nothing to do but to amuse themselves, to receive the homage of their lords, to be loved, and to be caressed."

"That part of the Kasbah," answered the hussar, laughing heartily, and patting the child familiarly on the shoulder, " was situated above the treasury the remains of which you have just seen."

Their cicerone then conducted them over the remaining parts of the Palace, showing them where had been the mosque, the great hall with its octagonal dome resting on marble columns, the halls of arms, the baths, the dens for lions and tigers, the enclosures for ostriches from the desert, the vine arbours, the powder-magazine, the pavilions for the tributary Beys who came periodically to pay their imposts and render an account of their administrations in their several provinces, the stables, and the various other important buildings — all surrounded, together with extensive gardens of wondrous beauty, by lofty walls bristling with cannon.

Finally St. Bertrand led them into the great hall, in which all the legal business of the State was transacted. Here the Dey sate on a throne of justice, surrounded by his nearest kinsmen, by his generals, and by his great officers of state, to hear and adjudicate upon the disputes and the crimes of his subjects.

Wilton remarked that when he was at Tunis

he saw the Bey presiding thus in his court at the country palace of Bardo.

As they came out of the Kasbah, the Marquis bowed low and took his leave, amid warm thanks for his courtesy.

"What an intellect!" exclaimed Olinda when he had left. "How clearly he explained every-thing, and what sensible remarks he made! It is cheering to meet sometimes a kindred spirit like this in one's dreary pilgrimage through life, with whom one can enjoy the privilege of inter-changing thoughts. He is literally bubbling with talent. Poor fellow! he appears sadly de-pressed in spirit at being buried alive, as he calls his existence in this place, instead of frequenting the gay *salons* of Paris, which he is so well fitted to grace. Is it not melancholy to see genius with no outlet for distinction?—to see it thus pitilessly hidden under a bushel, while pining to burst its fetters and leap into life?"

"He certainly does appear devoted to Paris life," Henry dryly replied, with a slight sneer of scorn. "Like most of his countrymen, he loves the gay distractions of the city, and feels miserably *triste* away from its giddy plea-sures. What a curse to Frenchmen must be the restless undomestic dispositions they in-herit!"

"That comes well from you, Henry," rejoined Olinda, smiling, "whom I hold to be the most

unsettled and most volatile of my acquaint-
ances."

"You are always accusing me, Olinda, of
versatility and want of stability of character,"
Henry retorted rather sorely. "You delight in
these taunts, but I should blush for myself were
your accusations well founded, and were I unable to enjoy the quiet society of my family fire-
side and of my female relations."

"Every man enjoys the society of his female
relations," she quickly retaliated, "unless indeed
he be lost to all sense of good feeling. So do
you, of course. So, no doubt, does the Marquis
de St. Bertrand."

"There I differ from you," replied Wilton.
"From what I have seen I judge him to be a
cold hardened man of the world, perhaps even
a confirmed *roué*, notwithstanding the plausible
cloak of amiability he wears and the smooth
professions he makes."

"That is an infamous calumny," Olinda
answered, half in badinage, "of which you
ought to be heartily ashamed. Were he a
Benedict he would become steady and sensible
enough. But he is too clever to endure contentedly the trammels that encircle him. He
wants occupation for his intellect—he wants a
field for his ambition."

"Why, Olinda, from the way you speak about
our new acquaintance and take his part," said

Henry, with a considerable dash of asperity, "any one would think he had made a deep impression upon you."

"And so he has, in one sense," she answered naively. "He is a charming companion, and actually saturated with genius. I could listen all day long to his witty and brilliant conversation."

"Just so, my poor girl!" Henry sorrowfully reflected, for this insensate passion to run blindly after talent always caused him bitter grief. "In your inexperience of life you look but to a showy outside. Too surely, I fear me, you will let some hollow superficial coxcomb like this befool you, and carry you away captive at his will!"

Descending to the Constantine Gate at the eastern side of Algiers, the party separated: Olinda, Miss Thornton, and Geraldine turning to their suburban villa on the heights of Isly, while Henry Wilton went to his quarters at the Hôtel de la Régence on Government Place.

CHAPTER IV.

THE VILLA ISLY.

IN the midst of picturesque glens and valleys, filled with a wondrous growth of the rarest trees — pomegranate, eucalyptus, palm, caroubier, bell'ombra, datura, standard magnolia, lemon, orange, peach, apricot, nectarine, fig, almond, banana, and vine, all flourishing in the open air—filled, in short, with every choice and beautiful product of the vegetable world—stands the pretty village of Isly, so called after the battle-field where the French, commanded by Marshal Bugeaud, defeated the armies of the Emperor of Morocco, who was marching to the assistance of Abd-el-Kader.

Here rises the villa of Alice Thornton, selected by Olinda, which commands splendid views from its lofty site, and nestles in bowers of surpassing luxuriance.

The snow-white glacier-like city, hanging on 'to the heights above, sweeps down to the waters of the bay—a mass of pure crystal set in the

deep emerald verdure of its villa-studded en-
virons; the heights of Mustapha, teeming with
wildly prolific tropical vegetation, stretch away
eastward; the hills of Bou-Zareah rise on the
west; while the bold range of the Lesser Atlas
Mountains bound the horizon to the south, and
enclose Algiers, together with the Sahel Hills on
which it stands, in a vast semicircle, terminated
on the west by the bold headlands of Chenoua,
and on the east by the towering spurs of the
Djurjura. A dense enveloping mantle of snow
clothes this bold range of the Lesser Atlas
Mountains throughout the winter, which does
not altogether disappear even during the
summer heats, small specks of unmolten white
hiding themselves in its deep chasms, that face
the north, away from the torrid rays of the
noonday sun.

The striking contrasts of the landscape—
masses of snow above, tropical vegetation beneath—recall to mind the lovely Borromean
Isles in the Lago Maggiore, whereon every
delicate product of the South and East flourishes
under the shadows of the ice-bound mountains
of the Simplon.

Graceful Moorish structures, adorned with
spacious marble courts, shady colonnades, plash-
ing fountains, gardens of roses, and cool leafy
groves—once the residences of corsair chieftains
and of the Dey's ministers of state—rise up

around, the walls of many covered to the top with dense luxuriant masses of the purple-flowering clematis.

A wide grassy terrace stretches round the villa, ornamented with beds of bright flowers, while the balmy breezes waft up delicious perfumes from the gardens below.

Sharply those mighty Djurjura peaks cut the clear blue canopy of heaven, and stand out in bold relief, though more than fifty miles distant, every projection and every indentation on the vast mass distinctly discernible.

Pure is the pellucid atmosphere of those sunny lands of the South! Sweet is their soft spring-time, with its warm invigorating power!

The wild wealth of vegetation, the beauteous flowers, the plains teeming with fertility, the genial glow of health, the unfading smiles of Nature, all well repay the traveller for leaving his chilly northern home to visit such genial climes.

No stifling fog spreads deadly gloom, no bitter cold wind blights with withering malignity, no darkling cloud casts dismal shade across the smiling landscape.

Olinda was sitting beneath the wide shady verandah that shuts out the scorching rays of the sun from the rooms inside the villa, and finishing a water-colour sketch, when Henry Wilton came and joined her.

He felt sad at heart, for, despite his efforts to stamp out the memories of the past, his thoughts would ever recur to the scene as they two ascended from the Marengo Gardens to the Kasbah, when Olinda had once more dashed his fondest hopes to the ground by declaring so decisively that she could never love him sufficiently to become his wife.

He felt sad at heart on her account as well as on his own. He dreaded the dangers that were only too certain to beset her in the future, owing to the ill-omened narrow groove into which she was drifting.

"Ay, poor thing! She thinks her talents and accomplishments would be thrown away on me, or on any one not a heaven-born genius," he sighed to himself in sadness while leaning over her shoulder, as she sat absorbed in the drawing, at which she continued to work after they interchanged recognitions on his entrance. "But, oh! what a dangerous course for woman to steer! What a rash, what a mad self-estimate! How readily may this poor young wayward creature be duped by a specious tongue and a hollow heart!—by such a man as that Marquis de St. Bertrand, or, worse still—for Raoul de St. Bertrand is a polished gentleman—by some scheming worthless adventurer, who may succeed in entrapping her under the mask of pretended mental endowments, not letting her

discover her fatal error until too late for repentance ! "

Sorely Wilton feared that her ardent impres-
sionable mind might be led away captive at the
will of the deceiver by such plausible means—
by the mere assumption of talent—causing her
to fall an easy prey to his wiles and snares.
Little could she realise, he knew, the unhappy
lot in store for her, wedded to such a man,
incapable of appreciating her worth, or of
comprehending what conjugal affection and
domestic felicity mean. Then would she discover, he thought—and bitterly to her cost—
her shortsighted folly in repelling a true and
loyal heart.

" Well, well, I fervently pray," he sighed,
" that so dire a misfortune may never befall the
dear girl—that she may never suffer degradation
and misery like this ! Such a fate would, of a
surety, soon crush her proud spirit and humble
her to the dust ! "

Such was the tender loving spirit in which
Henry mourned. Against his cousin he experienced no angry feeling for rejecting him—
rejecting him too on the invidious, humiliating
ground that he fell short of the ideal she had set
up to worship.

Others might have felt outraged, might have
become vindictive, at the mortifying defeat.
But his placid and amiable, yet at the same

time manly disposition scorned to harbour harsh thoughts like these against the woman he loved.

He judged her in pity, not in anger—in pity, moreover, tempered with love. He could therefore survey his position in a calm unprejudiced temper. And the survey forced him to own that Olinda was justified in seeking for one of her own intellectual calibre, in preference to himself. Far therefore from resenting, he undoubtingly acknowledged the justice of her *fiat*. He blamed her not. But he dreaded she would fail, and fail signally ; for he knew how few such exist in her station of life. He dreaded she would be betrayed and deceived ; that in seeking for too much, she would lose all.

He knew how large a proportion of the Upper Ten Thousand pass their lives engrossed with frivolity, with the turf, and too often with dissipation—habits they find next to impossible to shake off for longer than the first few years of wedded life. He loved her so unselfishly, and with so great devotion, he would have contentedly submitted to see her find a partner for life such as she had marked out, provided her happiness could be secured. But he believed not in her success. He felt assured that she would repent in tears of her too lofty aspirations.

Filled with these gloomy meditations, Wilton

was downcast in spirit, and remained long silent while standing behind his cousin, watching her brush, as it rapidly traversed the paper, guided by her skilful touch. Olinda likewise spoke not, wrapped in contemplation of her work.

The two cousins were on such a footing of intimacy that, since her first recognition of Wilton upon his arrival, she had continued engrossed in her occupation, as though forgetful he was there. Her vanity, however, prevented her from not remembering his presence. It led her, on the contrary, to rest under the delusion that he was absorbed in admiration of her handiwork, when his thoughts were far, far away, dwelling on the memories of the days gone past, and looking dreamily forward to the days to come.

At length she paused, and glancing upwards in his face of a sudden, she saw that care oppressed him. Then she said softly, with a gentle sympathetic smile : " You are cast down to-day, Henry, I can see. But you must not give way to this gloomy despondency. Remember your pledge."

" I do remember, Olinda, and I will faithfully keep my promise," he answered with firmness.

That his mind was depressed he had inadvertently betrayed, and he could not deny the fact, for had she not caught him in the very act ?

But the cause he sought to conceal, under the flimsy excuse that the intelligence received in a business letter had caused this feeling of momentary depression. Some foundation did exist for this pretext, still it was far from being the whole truth.

"Something is always going wrong in this perverse unlucky world of ours," he recommenced. "Burns was not so far wrong in his pathetic poem wherein he declares that 'Man is made to mourn.' Upon my word, I believe he was right in his summing-up of human life, for assuredly care and sorrow would seem our appointed lot from the cradle to the grave. Trouble and vexation persistently haunt us wherever we go."

It was most weak and injudicious of Henry to indulge in these thoughtless remarks, and own that trouble oppressed him, instead of trying to appear of good cheer; for he should have remembered that she knew of no sorrow on his mind, nor of any likely to arise, save the one, which could account for his saddened looks. He should have known that she must ascribe the change solely to regretful disappointment at being rejected by her. How could it occur to her mind that she herself was the object of his solicitude, or that he was anxiously contemplating what she might make her future become?

She naturally concluded that he was but endeavouring to deceive her, and that he yet mourned in secret over the old hidden grief, notwithstanding his promise to forget. Her womanly tact and kindliness, however, led her, for his sake, to dissemble, and appear to accept the truth of his assertion.

"I cannot take your dismal view of man's destiny here below, Henry," she replied, regarding him with affectionate solicitude.. "I hold that man has a far nobler mission to fulfil than to sit down in hopeless despair, and brood over real or imaginary troubles. In my belief he was constituted by his All-wise Creator for happiness, not for woe. I cannot ascribe to the Divine Being an arbitrary desire to plunge the creatures of His handiwork into a life of misery, as would seem distinctly implied by the words of the poet. The other day," she continued, "I wrote an answer to Burns's beautiful but lugubrious and, as I believe, most ill-considered, erroneous verses. Would you like to hear it?"

Wilton gallantly answered that any production emanating from her pen must be charming, and begged she would favour him with her reply.

Giving him a sweet smile, she tripped lightly indoors, and took from her escritoire the following poem.

MAN WAS NOT MADE TO MOURN.

Oh, no ! Man was not made to mourn
And have his heart-strings rudely torn.
His just and loving God above
Created him for joy and love,
And placed him in this world below,
With Heaven's reflected smiling glow
Bright burning from his brow serene
And lighting the terrestrial scene.
No grief, no care, no woe, no pain
Then brooded o'er the gladsome plain,
But all Creation joined to praise
The Mighty Author of their days;
While man diffused, high priest of joy,
Delights that knew not of alloy.
Bliss reigned supreme from morn to eve;
Man grieved not, nor had cause to grieve.
Then how came man to mourn ?   'Twas he
Brought woe on his posterity
By stretching sacrilegious hand
To disobey his Lord's command ;
Thus losing to his fallen race
The blessings of Jehovah's face.
Then darkness crept upon the earth,
Then Sin and Sorrow came to birth ;
The joyous smiles of Heaven had flown,
And man was left accursed—alone.
'Twas thus, degraded and forlorn,
That weeping Man began to mourn.
Still, if lost Man will humbly turn
To God above, he need not mourn.
The Mighty Arbiter of right
Wills not that Man in endless night
Should pine for all eternity.
He wills not that one soul should die.
He beckons to that heavenly bourn
Where none shall weep—where none shall mourn.

When she finished reciting, Wilton expressed the gratification her verses had afforded.

"Your view is most sensible and consoling," he said. "The Scottish Bard had converted me to believe in misery as the inevitable inheritance of poor fallen humanity. Now the clouds have been dispelled, to a large extent, by your soothing philosophy, which establishes, Burns notwithstanding, that unhappiness ought to be an abnormal condition, as being clearly opposed to the bountiful intentions of our Great Benefactor. To encourage and nurse melancholy thoughts is an evident act of folly, which a man of strong character should repudiate. Yet how difficult to reduce this theory into practice! How difficult to stare misfortune in the face with a light heart! Seldom do I succumb to weakness of this sort, and I have got a good lesson to-day to prevent a repetition."

This he said perceiving Olinda's want of faith in his assertions of amendment, and the suspicions she still entertained, which his pride induced him to try and dispel. Yet, in his heart, he inclined towards his first impressions, feeling more disposed to bewail his hard lot than to rest satisfied with her crumbs of comfort.

"Rest assured," she soothingly answered, "that in nine cases out of ten our miseries are self-inflicted, wholly arising from helplessness and want of common-sense. Rest assured that we can make or mar our own happiness. When man mourns, depend upon it, the fault is his own—he has but himself to blame."

"You speak sound wisdom, Olinda," he replied, striving to assume a gay and confident tone, "and I acknowledge what a mistaken estimate Burns and I formed of man's mission. But I see another poem in your hand. What may be the subject?"

"I shall be delighted to read it to you," she replied; "and I hope you will approve of it as well as of the last."

A SUMMER'S DAY.

When no breeze disturbs the brake,
When no ripple moves the lake,
When the sun shines bright on high
In the clear cerulean sky—
Oh! what bliss my bark to seek
Anchored in its lonely creek!
Borne upon the gliding skiff,
Under every towering cliff,
Every mountain, hill, and grove,
Joyous I delight to rove
Through the shadows that they throw
On the mirror-lake below.
Oh! how tranquil, how serene,
Is the fascinating scene!
How I love each spot around!
How I love each welcome sound!
The graceful swan, inflate with pride,
Dashes, triumphant, through the tide.
Amongst the trees the cushat dove
Coos the outpourings of his love.
The soaring kite, with piercing cry,
Sweeps in wide circles through the sky.
The thrush prolongs its mellow note;
The wild duck, scared up by the boat,

Rises aloft on rapid wings,
And flies away to distant springs.
The heron at the water's edge
Stands fishing in the reeds and sedge.
The greedy cormorants all day
Perch on the rocks and watch their prey.
The mews have left the ocean roar
To seek this solitary shore.
Returning from the mountain crest
The eagle soars down to his nest,
Built on a tree whose branches wide
Fling their reflections on the tide."
Fair are the many isles that break
The surface of this lovely lake,
Clothed with bright foliage to the shore,
Bold massive ruins towering o'er
Of abbey, fort, and dungeon keep,
That crown each verdure-covered steep.
Of this fair panoramic view
Reflected, sparkles every hue
On the smooth tide that softly laves
The rocks and forests with its waves.
The heart enthralled by crime and vice,
Changed to a block of senseless ice ;
The heart inured to scenes where strife
And toil and turmoil make up life ;
The heart to giddy pleasure slave
For false excitements madly crave.
They cannot tell the soothing bliss
Of peaceful calm retreats like this.
Nature her fairest charms displays
Unheeded to their soulless gaze.
The poet's or the painter's mind
Alone true heartfelt joy can find
In sights and sounds so bright, so gay,
Upon a glorious summer's day.

" Exceedingly pretty," Henry exclaimed.
" One's thoughts become involuntarily carried
away to the scenes you so vividly describe. What
would I not give to possess poetical feeling like

yours! Such a rare gift is indeed an invaluable blessing, that must ever prove a fruitful source of unmixed enjoyment."

"Undoubtedly it is a great boon," she artlessly replied. "While the mind continues absorbed in such pursuits one can feel no care, no ennui, no pining for the society of others; one feels independent of all the world. Life glides smoothly along, and time appears to fly only too rapidly past. How wretched must those feel who have no occupation for their mental faculties! How dull, how monotonous must be their dreary, useless existence!"

"Very true," he assented, though biting his lip and slightly colouring with mortification, for he could not but feel this remark was applicable to himself, whether so intended or not. "Still all the world cannot be geniuses," he continued. "Suppose we were all like you, for instance, witty and clever, you would not be appreciated half so much as now. You would then be no better than your neighbours, though your neighbours would be extremely proud of the change, or even if they had but half your abilities. What a mistake, Olinda," he added, "that you will obstinately persist in holding aloof from society, where you are fitted so well to shine, and to reap a golden harvest of admiration, distinction, and renown!"

"I want no such empty honours, Henry," she

replied with a smile, and a mantling blush that told what pleasure she derived from his praise. "To please the few intimate friends around me is all I desire; I ask for nothing more."

"But are you right in hiding your talents under a bushel?" he asked. "Remember the parable!"

"I think so," she said in reply, sweetly smiling again; for she was flattered, and strove not to conceal the feeling. "I think I am right in not rushing into snares and temptations."

"Not rushing into snares and temptations indeed!" he silently muttered, with a shrug of his shoulders. "That is just what you are doing, poor girl, though you know it not."

"Here is another of my poems," she added, "which I know you will like to hear."

THE MOUNTAIN RILL.

Tell me, joyous little rill,
Bounding gaily from the hill,
All the scenes, so blithe and gay,
Thou hast witnessed on thy way.

Tell me how, when first the sun
Views thee from the moorhill run,
Into marshy swamps o'erspread
Ere thy stream hath found a bed;
Wildfowl feed and lave and play,
Sure that man is far away.

Tell me how, when from the height
Trickles down thy wave so bright,
Arboured by the silver boughs
Birches spread from off the brows,

Gentle songsters of the wood
Welcome thy melodious flood;
Who, as though they would keep time
To the music of the chime,
Chorus with redoubled glee
As, fair rill, they gaze on thee.
On each giddy bough they throng,
Chanting thy glad course along;
And, when parched their tuneful throats
By the effort of their notes,
Haste to where thy golden brink
Offers a reviving drink.

Tell me how the speckled trout
Ever glide and sport about
Through each placid-bosomed breadth
Made by dam-like rock beneath,
Where thy silver waves so clear
Pause to rest in their career;
Or below the sparkling fall,
Showering o'er its rugged wall,
With intent unclosing eyes,
Wait the brightly coloured flies.

And, when nearer haunts of men,
Gladly gliding down the glen
Under darkly shadowed grove,
Welcome in the hour of love,
Tell me how thou oft hast caught
Glimpse of looks with rapture fraught—
Looks that from the fond eye dart,
Index of true lover's heart.

Tell me how thou half hast drowned
By thy waterfall's wild sound
Whispered accents of devotion,
Soft responses of emotion;
How the eye hath sought thy tide
Of shy maiden, turned to hide
From her swain the blush so sweet,
As he knelt before her feet;
How thy spray-mixed breeze did seek
Kisses from her lovely cheek—
Kisses which no mortal lip,
Save her own true love's, might sip.

Such thy course, fair rill, hath been
Ere thou cam'st to this ravine.
Faultless bliss was ever thine ;
Gaily thou didst dance and shine
Down each rock-paved valley hurled,
Joying in thy little world.

Yet the sombre pines above
Seemed thy rapture to reprove,
And to preach that gloom may dwell
Even in thy happiest dell.

Soon thy warm and blissful tide
To the ocean-wave must glide ;
In the surging billow's foam
Thou must find thy troubled home.

Then no longer may'st thou bring
Joy to every living thing ;
And, oblivion round thee cast,
Thou must be forgot at last.

"This pretty idea I have borrowed and worked up, as you no doubt perceive," observed Olinda, after receiving with manifest delight the encomiums of her cousin. " But I see nothing to be ashamed of in such a confession. I never could comprehend why poets should be debarred by the stern voice of public opinion, under the heaviest penalties of ridicule, from selecting a subject which had already formed a poetical theme, provided always that different phraseology and different treatment were employed. Indeed, our greatest poets have been accused of plagiarism, and sometimes with truth. Take, for instance, the beautiful opening of the Bride of Abydos :

' Know ye the land where the cypress and myrtle,' &c.

This is manifestly borrowed from the language
of the great German poet :

'Kennst du das Land wo die citronen blühn.'

Yet who thinks the worse of Byron for this
flagrant piece of literary pilfering, or admires
his poem one jot the less ? Even the immortal
Bard of Avon himself took large helpings from
the ideas of others, to convert them to his own
uses."

"That was poaching to some purpose," said
Henry. "Better than when he got caught in
the deer-park at Stratford, crossbow in hand.
By the way," he added, "the poacher must have
had fine times in Shakespeare's day, when no
report followed his shot, to arouse the keepers
and put them on his track."

Here Miss Thornton tripped nimbly out to
join them on the terrace, and Wilton took his
leave, after complimenting her on her youthful
agility.

He felt pride in the strength of mind he
vainly flattered himself he had displayed. He
had indeed abstained from any direct allusion to
the proscribed subject, yet had he suffered
Olinda to read his innermost thoughts. This
fact he could not realise. He thought he had
been so diplomatic as to succeed in persuading
her he was learning to submit and to efface her
image from his heart. As to the excuses he had

made, it appeared to him he could have said no less in reply to her observations about the despondency she had detected, and which it would have been vain to deny.

Fancying his explanation had convinced her, and that he had gained an advantage, he determined to keep it. He determined to give her a lesson—albeit a very gentle lesson—in humility. His devotion to her she had repaid by devotion to herself, and he determined she should feel that he entertained this conviction.

The surest method for bringing a headstrong woman to reason—especially when one would make her pine to regain the homage and love she has lost—is to exhibit just the slightest *soupçon* of studied distant reserve and formality.

By gentleness alone can woman be won, if she can be won at all. The last resource of angry hostility, or the strong hand of authority, generally proves a fatal blunder. Woman may easily be led, but you can only drive her—above all, when of an obstinate self-opiniated temperament—at the sacrifice of her affections. She may and probably will submit, but better would it be that she refused. If evil-minded, she will hate the man who forces and drives her into reluctant submission. Outwardly she may caress the hand, but inwardly she will burn to drive a dagger into the heart.

Henry well knew these characteristics of the

female breast. He knew the other sex require tact in management, its employment being modified according to the widely divergent circumstances that arise. Overweening gentleness and want of decisiveness on the one hand, or harshness and dogged opposition on the other, serve but to produce the effect, in most cases, of confirming woman's determination to continue her policy of resistance, once she has taken her standpoint prepared to do battle.

Into either of these courses Wilton was too politic to fall. He resolved to display neither weakness nor ill-feeling, yet he would assert his independence and prove that he was her slave no longer. He would prove that his spirit was not bruised and broken, as she chose to believe.

The means he adopted were simple but effectual. No word escaped his lips to let her think his cheerfulness while conversing with her had been feigned. No look of irritation appeared on his brow. But, in lieu of the wonted familiar leave-taking, he made her a polite formal salutation, that faithfully performed its mission, drawing hot blushes of surprised mortification to her cheek. She perceived the slight, perceived it was intentional, perceived the cause, and resented it bitterly.

But he could not comprehend the extent of his unkindness, for his aim in humbling was to win her. Love, in fact, prompted the deed; for even still, hopeless though his prospects appeared, he indulged expectations of ultimate success; and he believed that by humbling her, although by such gentle means, he was adopting the surest method to work out the ultimate realisation of his desires.

The conviction that Olinda had converted him by her arguments, and proved to him the fallacy of continuing to urge his suit, had already become dissipated, to make room again for the old passion with all its former force.

Into such infatuated weaknesses and extravagant contradictions does Love betray his helpless votaries!

He would still kindly persist in hoping against hope. He was still all for her. She was still all for herself.

CHAPTER V.

IN forcible contrast with the formal uninterest-
ing French architecture in the lower part of
Algiers, that runs parallel to the sea—and to
make room for which the fine old Djenina
Palace of the Turkish Deys, together with its
beautiful gardens of Bab-el-Oued, were ruthlessly swept away—the ancient Moorish and
Arab portion of the city rises aloft up the steep
hillside, clothed in all its quaint originality,
glistening white and bright in the warm blaze
of sunlight.

Singularly striking is this weird old Arab
quarter, where the jealous, narrow-minded, sensual natives seclude themselves and their women
in their outer-world-excluding dwellings, that
only communicate with the street by a carefully
guarded door in the external wall. Strange
appear the ghostlike women that flit through
this mysterious region, enveloped in white burnouses gathered closely round the figure, none

of the face visible save wild scorching black eyes, that flash with the impetuous ardour of hot Southern blood above the veils that conceal the rest of their swarthy features. But though they appear so careful to conceal their features from the opposite sex, some will, on occasion, delight the favoured by seizing an opportunity, unobserved, to open their shroud-like costumes so as to display their forms—too often coarse, unwieldy, and repulsive—which are encased in richly embroidered trousers drawn in at the ankle over *papouche* slippers, and in handsome zouave jackets laden with golden braid, the whole adorned with a mass of pendant gold charms and trinkets.

But what hard, ungentle, unfeminine, unlovable faces! What heavy beetling eyebrows, painted in a broad black band across the forehead with *afsah!* What revolting, filthy-looking, unwashen eyelids, laden with *kohuhl!* What strange finger-nails, stained bright red with *henna!*

And their minds and souls?

Ah, well, poor things! Such questions awaken sad reflections. They fill us with pity for the thousands in Mahometan lands who live and die in the grossest ignorance, yet whose worldly position would seem to entitle them to a better fate.

How little superior, alas! are these poor

enslaved benighted beings to the wild savage of the forest, or even to the beasts that perish!

The region where live these dark-eyed houris is indeed fair to behold from afar, where only its masses of shining whitened walls can be distinguished; but within it is full of all uncleanness, literally as well as figuratively. Here gross sensuality and crime reign supreme amid the depraved debased inhabitants! Here deadly fever often gathers a rich harvest in the badly built, badly drained, badly ventilated habitations.

Wealth and penury, luxury and misery, pride and humiliation, side by side!

Hard by squalid loathsome dwellings of the poor arise the far-extending white walls of palatial residences belonging to the rich, stretching along the narrow foot-passages, over which the arched and vaulted houses often meet above.

Here, shut out from vulgar gaze, the indolent natives pass their lives, surrounded by profuse magnificence, wasting their days in ignorance, frivolity, and vice.

In one of these luxurious palaces a lovely young girl was reclining upon a soft velvet couch, fanned by her attendant Negress, and sipping coffee from a *fendjal*—a small cup made of slender egg-shell china, and coming to a point at the bottom. A cushion of rich crimson

velvet supported her head, while beneath the
hip and shoulder on which she lay small pillows
of the softest eider-down, covered in thick brocaded satin, were carefully placed, to prevent
her from being incommoded by the weight of
even her light sylph-like form pressing upon
these parts of her body.

Clouds of incense-like perfume, that arose
from fragrant woods which were burning on a
chafing-dish in the centre of the apartment,
slowly floated in wreaths around her head, and
she inhaled from time to time the refreshing
odours of the delicious geranium-scent distilled
by the Trappist Fathers at the Monastery of
Staouéli.

The massively furnished chamber in which
she reposed opened upon a wide verandah running round the inner walls of the house, above a
spacious court that lay stretched out below, and
where gigantic orange and lemon trees, their
golden fruit hanging on the same boughs as
their perfumed flowers, towered up aloft and
flung grateful shade into the apartments of the
harem.

In this court joyous shoals of gold-fish disported through crystal pools supplied by icy
water that flowed down from distant hills,
in whose pellucid waves shone reflected the
brilliant colours of rich and choice flowering
plants, spread around in lavish profusion, and

perfuming the air with their delicious fra-
grance.

Gushing fountains showered their glittering
spray over the fair scene, imparting delightful
coolness to the wooing breeze, and soothing the
ear with mellifluous cadence.

Light and gracefully constructed aviaries stood
in shady nooks, whose trelliswork sides were
clothed in hanging festoons of creeping plants,
and whose bright-plumaged inmates poured
forth from their tiny throats a perpetual chorus
of sweet soothing notes.

Dreamy gossamer architecture, with elaborate
ornamentation—so dear to the Moor—adorned
this lovely court, out of which wide flights of
unsullied marble steps led up to the mysterious
regions of the harem. The lofty walls were
encrusted with enamel of the brightest and most
varied colours, and with the most delicate lace
and shawl patterns of decoration, whose skilfully
harmonized tints shed a mellowed subdued rich-
ness over the fairy scene.

Through exquisitely sculptured archways lay
the way to the far-extending pleasure-grounds,
whose darkling groves of choice umbrageous
trees from many lands, watered by bounding
rills, and affording through their leafy boughs
charming vistas of the deep blue sea far below ;
whose bowers of roses, and whose terraces laden
with blossom, with sculptured urns and vases,

and with marble statuary, completed a terrestrial paradise of unruffled enjoyment.

Such was the abode of beauty and luxury that had ever delighted the eyes of the lovely Azzahra from early childhood—who dreamed not, in her simple innocence, that any spot on earth could be so fair. Here the days of her youth were passed. Here she had grown to border on woman's estate. Here had concentred all her dreams and aspirations after happiness. Here she was content to live, content to die.

Such hitherto had been her pure maidenly experience of life.

But a change was coming over the spirit of her aimless existence. A shadowy cloud of thought and anxiety was perceptible upon the fair young brow, where, till now, the smiles of peaceful contentment had maintained undivided sway.

The high-spirited girl had begun to pine for the fruit of the Tree of Knowledge, that her eyes might be opened so as to know good from evil.

What countless calamities has this Tree of Knowledge entailed upon the human race! what happiness has it turned into misery! what love into hatred! what innocence into guilt and crime!

Were only good derived from partaking of its fruit, how thankful would the heart feel for the blessings conveyed! But, alas! is such the case? Does not what is learned too often unsettle and disturb the mind, plunging man into vain speculations and doubts he strives to stifle, but which persist in rising above the surface, irrepressible, all-powerful, and loudly demanding solution?

In like manner are not the minds of the masses led astray and corrupted by vain spurious ambition, through the insight the fruit they have partaken of confers regarding a higher life than theirs in the classes above them, making them discontented with their lot, and eager to pull down those to whose height they cannot reach, with the purpose of usurping their places?

Without proper controlling counteracting influence, such dangers attend on the eating of this fruit—so fair to look on, and so pleasant to taste.

Imperative is the necessity
For education—for a ruling power
To regulate the mind in early youth,
Whilst it is pliable and void of strength;
To hollow out a channel for the thoughts,
Down which they may flow on to fields of bliss,
With all their early strength and innocence,
Pure and unsullied as some crystal brook!

Yet, oh! how few can comprehend aright,
That are entrusted with the charge of youth,
The nature of their great responsibility!

How few direct and train in fitting form
The tender sproutings of the sapling plant !
How many force the intellect alone
For superficial show in after-life ;
Neglecting all that moulds the character,
And stamps it with the marks of the Divine ;
Cultivating not those better parts of man—
The heart, the disposition, and the soul!

Can we then wonder that the human mind,
Left thus undisciplined and uncontrolled
In what concerns its everlasting peace,
Which by its nature cleaves to guilt and sin,
Should soon be overgrown with rankest weeds,
And that the vilest passions should spring up,
Fierce, powerful, and irresistible ?

Wrapped in deep unwonted reflection Azzahra reclined, attired in elaborately embroidered deep-blue satin trousers drawn in at the ankle, in a crimson satin *djedaboli* vest heavily laden with golden embroidery, and in a richly braided *r'lila* jacket of purple velvet. Upon her head a blue velvet *chachia* cap was gracefully posed, from beneath which hung down her rich black hair, tied behind her back with ribbons of red silk shot with gold. Her delicate hands were laden with immense rings of roughly cut precious stones in coarse silver setting, manufactured by the confraternity of jewellers at the eyry-like village of Illali, in the Kabyle Mountains. On her arms she wore *m'sais*, or bracelets; and on her ankles bangles, called *m'kais;* while from her neck, and from the belt round her waist, hung

festooned masses of golden chains and orna-
ments, clustered in glittering profusion.

As soon as she had finished her coffee she
clapped her hands, and the Negress glided back
noiselessly into the apartment. She presented
to her mistress a small open-work vessel of
silver filigree-work resembling an egg-cup, in
which Azzahra placed the footless *fendjal*,
pointed like an egg at the lower end.

This Soudan girl was descended from slaves
who had been dragged in bondage to Algiers
by the dreaded robber tribe of Touaregs, and
sold to the Turks, before the French conquest
of the country.

These ferocious Touaregs—the Pirates of the
Desert—were as terrible on land as the Corsairs
were at sea. They watched habitually for these
unsuspecting victims going to collect salt at
the Sebkhas, or salt lakes of the Sahara, when,
pouncing on them and seizing them unawares,
they led them off as prizes, to be sold into
captivity in the Algerian slave-market.

The massive sphinx-like features of the Black
bore the stamp of benevolence, and her manners
were soft and engaging. To her young mistress,
over whom she exercised unbounded influence,
she was deeply, passionately devoted.

"A wondrous change has come to me of
late, Kredoudja," murmured Azzahra, in a tone
of dreamy despondency, as she handed back

her cup to the Soudanese. "It fills me with dread."

"Such, alas! have I observed in sorrow," replied the serving-girl, not presuming to inquire the cause.

"Kredoudja," her mistress mournfully proceeded, "I begin to feel miserable and discontented. The aspect of everything seems changed, and changed for the worse. All around seems to have lost its beauty and its charm. What can be the cause, Kredoudja? Here I am surrounded by every luxury and enjoyment that a devoted parent's love can provide, or that woman's heart can sigh for. Everything combines to make me contented and happy, yet I am most discontented and most unhappy. You think me unwise, Kredoudja, for harbouring such thoughts, and so, unquestionably, I am ; but you know that over our feelings we can exercise no control. They become our masters, and we their slaves. I pine madly, Kredoudja, for occupation—for action—for life! I pine to move in that great world that is now so cruelly shut out from view! I pine to shake off this degraded contemptible existence to which the women of Mahometan lands are doomed! I pine to burst my chains!—I pine to be free! Oh, Kredoudja, you know not how galling has become this life of serfdom and bondage—this life of ignoble, indolent, objectless, soulless inactivity! You know not how I chafe at my prison-bars, and how I should exult at shaking off the cruel fetters I wear!"

"The problem is easily solved," sadly rejoined the faithful Negress, "and the cause of this transformation easily traced back to its source. Long have I dreaded that the knowledge and the accomplishments you are acquiring from your Christian instructress would but unsettle your mind—would make you pant for change—would make you despise your own people and your father's house—would make you despise even the Prophet of God and His holy Religion! These are the causes that have brought about your altered condition, turning your happy home into a prison-house. Alas! that I should have lived to see the day that brings to you this dire calamity! And do these hollow superficial advantages compensate for all you lose? Of what avail are they, or will they ever be, to one living, as you are destined to live all the days of your life, in seclusion from the world? Doubtless they cheer in the hours of solitude, but are they not, on the other hand, a dangerous snare? Must not a desire to have her acquirements known and appreciated awaken within woman's breast a yearning for the society of others, a desire to be admired and praised, such as fills the hearts of the brazen, unblushing, barefaced daughters of Europe?"

"My father's wives, and my brothers and sisters, give me their admiration and praise," Azzahra answered evasively; "that suffices."

Kredoudja crept cautiously to the verandah outside, upon which the doors of the other harem apartments opened, to see whether any listened. When satisfied that none overheard she returned, and whispered in Azzahra's ear: "All are jealous. They like you not—ay, they hate you—because you are superior to themselves, and because your father loves you best. Outwardly they make a pretence of admiring you and praising you, to propitiate his favour, but at heart they love you not."

"Too well I know this," Azzahra said in sadness. "Too deeply I feel they are in a hostile league against me in secret, and would even wish me dead. Oh! it is so dreary to be left thus, with none to care for me, save my father, and he remains so rarely at home. Were it not for you, Kredoudja, and for my birds and my flowers, mine would indeed be a dismal lot, notwithstanding all this pomp and magnificence, an object of aversion as I am to all my kindred. Oft I fancy those I see around are far happier than myself, for they have no ambition, no aspirations after better things, no refinement of feeling to disgust them with the dull monotony of their despicable, unintellectual existence. To them this colourless life of imprisonment can have no horrors—can be no curse, as, alas! it is to me.   My flowers and my dear birds I passionately love, but they suffice not to satisfy my cravings after something worthy to live for.   My heart and my head both tell me this is not life—that I am destined for better, for more glorious things."

"But reflect, my dear young mistress," interposed Kredoudja, deeply scandalised at the whirlwind pace with which Azzahra's ideas were rushing ahead, and at her evident desire to shake off all trammels and restraint—"reflect that our Holy Prophet in the ever-blessed Koran forbids us to copy the shameless daughters of the accursed Christians, expressly enjoining this secluded life for the women of the Faithful."

"Then he enjoins what is a deep degradation to the sex," bitterly retorted Azzahra.   "The inventor of such a religion ought to be heartily ashamed of himself."

For some moments she remained abstracted in thought.   Then she resumed.

"Perhaps you are right, Kredoudja," she said, "in thinking I should have been happier reared up in the ignorance of our race, with no mental culture, with no ambitious aspirations.   Perhaps, when woman is doomed to our debased condition, it is better she should know nothing of the honoured and happy position enjoyed by her more favoured sisters in other lands—better not to know the arts by which they secure the homage and esteem of men."

"Ah, my dear young mistress, you know not what you say," interrupted the Negress in alarm. "You know not how dangerous to those who desire to walk in the paths of virtue are such soft insidious arts. They are but a deceitful, treacherous stumblingblock, believe me — too prone, alas! to overthrow woman into the depths of irretrievable ruin and despair. And as to this life of seclusion, it will not always continue. Your father will bestow you in marriage on some wealthy chieftain of our own race; perhaps shortly too—who can tell? Then you will be your own mistress; you will be free from the jealousies and the smothered hatred that beset you here; you will have a husband to love you and to realise every desire of your heart."

"Speak not to me of the unholy, accursed unions of our brutalised sensual race!" ejaculated Azzahra, springing up excitedly and stamping her pretty little slippered foot upon the floor. "What happiness, think you, could I experience in sharing with others a husband's affections? Could I brook seeing the man I love clasp others in close fond embraces, imprint warm kisses on their false smiling lips, pour into their delighted ears vows of passionate devotion?— could I witness all this and not even presume to raise my voice in remonstrance? Never could I submit to such grovelling humiliation; never could I endure having the love which should be mine, and mine only, shared by jealous and perhaps triumphant rivals!"

She walked out on the verandah, to hide from Kredoudja the tears that the contemplation of such a bitter sacrifice brought to her eyes; and leaned over the balustrade, to admire the rich foliage below, to inhale the perfume of orange and citron blossoms, and to feel the cool bright spray from the fountains light upon her cheek. Then, with a deep sigh, she went back and flung herself again upon her couch.

"Oh, Kredoudja! how I envy those happy Christians," she said, "who are coequal with their husbands, trusted by them, loved and cherished by them; favoured beings, to whom their lords devote their whole heart and soul, to whom they are bound by indissoluble bonds, who are their companions and friends as well as their lovers! This would be bliss indeed, to be joined thus in the holiest ties to him one loves, to be the constant subject of his undivided care and solicitude; though two outwardly, to be so united as to be but one flesh, according to the beautiful doctrine of the Christians! Better, oh! how far better, not to wed at all than to wed in unhappiness! Here my kind good father gives me pure heartfelt love, and gratifies my slightest wish; but in a new home how long could I count on my affection being returned? I should but exchange one prison for another, and peradventure the new one would be worse than the first; for what should I have in common with a gross-minded, untutored consort —with such an one as my father would probably select to be my partner for life? I should but regard him with scornful aversion; I should but sigh to be united, instead, to one of the refined and polished sons of Europe!"

"Ah! these refined and polished strangers are as hollow and treacherous as the grave," interrupted the serving-girl, for she trembled to see her young mistress commence to walk in the misguided footsteps of her ill-fated mother. "You know them not; you judge them, I sorely fear me, through the prejudiced accounts you have heard from Madame Lagrange. She it is who has unsettled your mind by describing to you the great world without, in which you are destined never to move, instead of confining her attention to the duties assigned her—the superintendence of your studies, with a view to prepare and fit you for the life you will be forced to lead. Oh! what a dire misfortune that your unhappy mother insisted, as a parting request, on your receiving this ill-omened European education, and that your father was weak enough to comply blindly with her wishes and give her that fatal promise! Did he know that you, like your poor mother, thus regard the Franks with favour, whom he abhors with such deadly hatred, and that you could meditate even for one moment espousing one of the accursed race, he would disown you and never see you more, deeply though he loves you now!"

"Of that I am well aware," was the reply, "and the conviction sorely grieves me, because I would not for worlds inflict pain on my beloved parent by such a step. Yet, even to please him, I would not wed the wealthiest Moor or Arab in Algiers. What I pine for is freedom, not the serfdom of marriage. Oh, what would I not give for romance!" she continued, rising again and pacing her chamber with excited steps. "Give me wild adventure, hairbreadth escapes, scenes even of battle and strife—anything sooner than this unvarying detested imprisonment! Give me the untrodden solitudes of the Atlas, and the glorious unfettered freedom of the Desert!"

As she concluded, an infirm old man leaning on a staff advanced into the apartment, clad in filthy rags, at sight of whom Azzahra veiled her face, and the two girls fled precipitately, deeming him some audacious intruder, for they failed to recognise in the lowly poverty-stricken form before them the proud and wealthy owner of the house. He was disguised as a mendicant

Marabout, and presented a most repulsive aspect. His long dishevelled hair fell in matted masses over his forehead; his feet were encased in tattered wayworn *papouches ;* in one hand he held the strong stick that supported his tottering frame, and from the other hung a chaplet of beads for counting his prayers while he performed his devotions.

As soon as he spoke and called after them Azzahra detected the sound of her father's voice, whom for months she had not beheld; and she eagerly rushed back to embrace him and welcome his return, although his reason for assuming the loathsome disguise he appeared in passed her comprehension.

Selim Mustapha was a tall, powerful, strongly built man, with a beetling brow and a villainous sensual expression of countenance, that but too truly reflected his black, morose, bloodthirsty nature; yet one redeeming characteristic distinguished him, which was deep, devoted, passionate love for his child Azzahra.

The girl's mother he had loved and prized more than all his other wives; but her jealous rivals had accused her, although most falsely, as he unhesitatingly believed, of carrying on an intrigue, many years before, with a French officer quartered in Algiers, during one of his long absences in the interior. He had always refused to give credence to the scandal; but, nevertheless, he had been forced to discard her at their repeated solicitations, for by her marked levity of conduct she had given considerable grounds for the accusation, and had laid herself open to their aspersions on her character.

Now he prized his daughter for her cherished sake, and sought by devotion to her offspring to make atonement to the divorced wife for the cruelty with which he had treated her. He well knew that this marked preference caused secret exasperation amongst the rest of his household, for which reason he longed to remove the fair bright girl from amongst the spiteful narrow-minded clique, so far inferior to her in every respect. In deference to the last farewell desire of the child's mother—a desire he could never account for—he had reared Azzahra under the care of a Christian preceptress, and given her an education which he felt elevated her so much that she was thrown away amidst such an un-lettered circle, who were unable to appreciate her great worth.

She could not, she ought not to be happy, he argued, in their society, and he longed to make her happy.

It was with profound joy, therefore, that he overheard his child declare that she pined for the solitudes of the Atlas and for the freedom of the Desert.

This was the life he loved himself, and he

rejoiced to learn that she loved it too. In the
Desert she had been born ; she had been reared
in early infancy a Child of the Desert, and a
Child of the Desert she should continue.

What a triumphant refutation of his lost wife's
calumniators, who asserted that Azzahra was not
his child, this brave outburst of sentiment proved,
he thought, carried away by the blind unreasoning impulsiveness of his race! How clearly it
demonstrated that the proud girl was a true
Child of the Desert, that she was an undoubted
daughter of the Bedouins, and inherited through
himself their wild traditions and instincts! How
these heroic feelings stamped her, Allah be
praised! as distinct from the delicately reared,
tame, spiritless daughters of Europe! Oh! had
his wife been in reality false—did one drop of
Frankish blood course through Azzahra's veins
—how he would abhor the child and spurn her
from his side! But never more would he allow
even the faintest foul suspicion regarding his
beloved offspring to cross his thoughts, for to
his mind these generous noble exclamations
were ample and conclusive evidence.

By what a slight breath of wind can the mind
of man be turned, alas! where love intervenes.
True is the saying, "What we desire we easily
believe." How readily are the thoughts directed
into whatever channel we wish them to follow!
By what slender foundations are our proudest

superstructures supported! How blind and how helpless we are!

Had Selim Mustapha reflected calmly for one moment, he would have discovered the futility and absurdity of such logic, for might not these instincts which he gloried to find in his child be inherited as well from the mother's side as from the father's? Might they not have been cultivated and engrafted where she had passed her early childhood?

Firm in his belief, however, he pressed the fair young creature fondly to his heart, and imprinted loving warm kisses on her smooth soft brow.

"Bravely said, my child!" he exclaimed with pride, lifting himself up erect, and flinging away the staff on which he had been supporting his apparently enfeebled limbs. "You are worthy to be my offspring! You are worthy to be the descendant of a long line of conquering chieftains! You are worthy of your noble race! You are worthy to be a Child of the Desert! And can you act bravely as you have spoken, my daughter? Will you come along with your father to the depths of the Sahara? Will you live amid the fruit-trees and vines, amid the date-palms of the Oases? Will you, without regret or repining, surrender all this splendour, with which you have been surrounded from childhood, to share with a parent his hard-

ships and dangers; to mingle in scenes of turmoil and strife; to join, it may be, in the fray of
the battle; to be a Child of the Desert?"

"Oh, with what delight!" she exclaimed in
the passionate impulsive rapture of her girl's
heart. "Such is the free roving life I should
love. Besides with you, my dear father, I could
anywhere be happy. How much more then
wandering without restraint over the trackless
wilds, unfettered as the pure unsullied air I
breathed!"

"Spoken like a heroine, Azzahra!" he cried,
exultant at her brave spirit, while tears of joy
started from her eyes as he clasped her in his
arms once more. "Allah bless you, my beloved daughter! How you recall every look,
every lineament, of your adored mother! How
your heart, like hers, is in the land of the
free, amid our noble untamed nomad tribes of
the far South! Your poor, poor mother! Ah!
where is she now?—what is she saying?—what
is she thinking?—what is she doing?"

And the proud, hard, strong man flung himself upon the ground, covering his face with his
hands.

Azzahra then crept over, and, kneeling down
beside him, laid her hand with a gentle touch
upon his shoulder, as she looked softly into his
weeping eyes.

"Oh, my father!" she plaintively murmured,

"how I should love to behold my adored mother once more—once more to see her sweet, benign, loving smile, which I so well remember from the days of my childhood—once more to kneel at her feet and invoke her blessing! Oh! is she never to return, my father?—never more to gladden our hearts?"

"Never, my daughter!" he replied, sorrowfully shaking his head. "Even now in my heart I believe her innocent of the guilt they laid to her charge. I believe she loved me with too deep, too devoted affection to inflict such a grievous wrong. But they made me drive her away from my side, a divorced, a spurned outcast! She is gone—gone for ever! But you I have got, my treasured Azzahra, and well you compensate for all my heavy afflictions!"

"Oh, my father! my dearly beloved father! why not relent and summon back my adored mother, even now?" earnestly pleaded the weeping girl. "If you still love her, if you still believe her innocent of those terrible accusations, why continue to let her remain a byword and a reproach?"

"Impossible, my child!" he replied with firmness, yet in a voice choking through emotion. "I should be a very mockery and a laughing-stock unto mine own house. How could my women honour or respect me, how care to preserve even an outward semblance of virtue before me, were such foolish heedless levity forgiven as that of which your poor dear mother was guilty? What would I not give to incline to the side of pity and mercy! What would I not give to receive her back to my arms! But, alas! alas! I must not yield; I dare not indulge in such fatal weakness."

"My beloved father!" she continued, nothing daunted by his refusal, "I will relate to you a tale, by which you will see what dangers and misfortunes come from the vindictive harshness of a husband, and what blessings follow when he hearkens to the voice of persuasion and exercises merciful clemency.

"THE LADY AND THE LIONESS.

"One day the fair Mariyah was summoned to the presence of her husband, who exclaimed in cruel and heartless tones, 'In the name of Allah I divorce you; you are wife of mine no longer!'

"Mariyah perceived by the forbidding sternness with which he spoke that remonstrance would be vain, and that he would never revoke the unjust decree by taking her back to his bosom; so the pure loving wife departed for ever from her happy home, to wander an outcast on the face of the earth.

"After roaming about for some time through wild and desert tracts, she discovered a cavern which seemed a secure retreat against all

dangers; but on entering she perceived a
lioness inside, at the sight of which she became
struck with consternation. The fawnings of the
animal upon her, however, quickly dissipated
her apprehensions, and she then comprehended
that these acts of fondness were not without
meaning. The lioness, very large with young
and unable to bring forth her litter, clearly begged
for a service. That Mariyah hastened to perform.

"After the beast was thus happily delivered
her gratitude was not confined to momentary de-
monstrations. From that day forth she failed not
to bring and lay at Mariyah's feet a sufficient supply of daily food so long as her whelps detained
her in the cavern. When she had reared them,
Mariyah ceased to see her, and was reduced to
seek for her own subsistence. But she could
not often go out without seeing gangs of kid-
napping Touaregs, who at last seized her and
made her a slave, intending to sell her at Algiers
to the Turks. But seeing a party of the Dey's
soldiers marching towards them through the
Chiffa Pass, as they were descending from
Medeah, they clambered up the Mouzaïa heights,
dragging their captive along with them.

"There they tied her to the trunk of a tree,
intending to come back for her when all danger
of pursuit was over. But the Algerine troops
dashed up the hill after them, and with such
good success that they captured the leader, after

an exciting chase through the mountains. This
man's heart smote him, after he was cast into
prison at Algiers, when he thought how his
hapless victim was perishing from starvation.
Besides, he hoped that he would be lightly dealt
with by the authorities in consideration of his
delivering so much beauty into their hands.
Soldiers were forthwith sent to the spot indi-
cated, where they were amazed to find her alive
and unhurt, though surrounded by panthers and
lions, who dared not even approach because a
lioness with several young lions stood guard at
her feet. At sight of the soldiers the lioness
withdrew a little, to leave them, as it were, at
liberty to unbind her benefactress.

"Mariyah related to the men her romantic
adventure with the animal, whom she recognised
immediately; and when she was loosed from her
bonds, and the escort were preparing to conduct
her to Algiers, the lioness once more fawned
greatly upon her, seemingly full of sorrow at
seeing her depart. The report given by the
soldiers to their superiors made them understand that they could not, without appearing
more savage than lions, help granting liberty to
a woman whom Heaven had so visibly taken
under its protection. Furthermore, they conveyed a message to the husband, urging him to
take back his good and beautiful wife; and
shortly afterwards they had the satisfaction of

learning that he had relented and yielded to
their entreaties, returning thanks to God, who
had put such good and blessed counsel into
their hearts."

After she had finished she laid her hand again
on her father's shoulder, and looked in his face
with a soft beseeching smile, pleading her cause
thus with " silent eloquence." But she failed to
move the heart of Selim Mustapha, or to shake
his resolve.

"Name not this again, beloved child," he
gently though firmly exclaimed. "It cannot,
it must not be."

"So you will come, my daughter," he continued, after some moments of thoughtful silence,
"to brave the hardships and dangers of the
Desert? Well, you must keep yourself in readi-
ness; it will not be many days ere we shall
have to depart."

The proud spirited girl told her father, in reply,
that he would find her prepared and eager for
the journey whenever he should summon her to
start.

"Doubtless you wonder, Azzahra," he continued, "at beholding me thus habited in mean
attire. I am forced to adopt degrading disguise
like this, else I dared not have entered Algiers
to-day to pay you this hurried visit. Our loathed
conquerors would have recognised me through

their perjured spies—spies, too, of our own race
—whom they employ in our midst to betray us,
bribed by their accursed gold. Had they discovered my identity, they would have compelled
me to account for my transgression of their orders
by quitting Algiers without authorised permission from the Government, and would have
watched me so closely for the future that I dared
not leave again for months to come.

"But, Allah be praised! my absence while far
away in the desert wilds was not observed, nor
was I detected returning, thanks to these foul
disgusting rags. Despite the tyrannical devices
of my enemies, I have reached my dwelling in
safety, and they will never learn of my long
sojourn away in the far Sahara. Oh! did they
but know the truth—did they suspect I came disguised in this fashion to elude and befool them
—what rage would seize upon the souls of the
Christian dogs!

"It is upon an important mission I have
arrived, as well as to see you, dear Azzahra;
and the moment my affairs permit I shall start
again for the Sahara."

"Reckon on me," his daughter repeated; "I
shall count the minutes until we leave. But
will not you allow Kredoudja to come too?" she
pleaded. "The faithful girl is such a devoted attendant, and I am so accustomed to have her near
my person, that we should be wretched apart."

"Your waiting-maid shall go with us, my child," he replied, smiling, and gently smoothing with his large rough hand Azzahra's rich raven tresses. "This request I grant with the greater pleasure, for the young woman possesses the appearance of prudence and steadiness beyond her years. As you will be forced of necessity to discontinue your studies while we are absent, which I faithfully promised your dear mother should not be neglected, I rejoice that one should always be near you whom I can well trust, and who will be your confidential companion throughout the varied scenes of our wanderings. Remember, you will find your new life a great change. You will miss your surroundings. You will miss your admirable instructress, who teaches you so well how to employ with profit your leisure hours.

"Oh! how I hope she has discharged her duty faithfully, without betrayal of her trust by casting opprobrium on our Moslem habits enjoined by the Prophet, or by polluting your ears with praise of the accursed Giaour!

"With deep forebodings I entrusted your education to the care of a Christian; but the woman promised fairly that she would not tamper with your religion, and, moreover, your mother's request was urgent that you were not to grow up in what she styled the gross ignorance and absence of occupation that prevail in

our Mahometan harems. Wherefore she entertained these strange scruples I could never discover; but her wishes I hold sacred, and ever
shall do so unto my life's end."

"Madame Lagrange is too good and too honourable to break her word," Azzahra answered;
"she never once attempted to interfere with my
religious belief."

This was shameful prevarication on the part
of Azzahra. Madame Lagrange, it is true, had
never openly and directly forced Christianity
upon her pupil; but she had taken every opportunity of descanting insidiously on the debasing
errors of the Mussulman religion, and on the
beauty and holiness of her own faith.

Selim Mustapha, however, felt satisfied with
his daughter's denial. "Heaven be praised!"
he fervently ejaculated. "After that declaration I know how to secure your happiness.
On our return from the Desert I will find
you a husband worthy of you among our own
people, as soon as you have completed your
studies."

To his dismay Azzahra remained silent without manifesting any token of satisfaction.

"Why this silence, my daughter?" he inquired anxiously, surprised that she betrayed
none of the delight which Eastern women experience on hearing of their betrothal.

"Oh, my father!" she pleaded with passionate

earnestness, "what sympathy or love could I feel for one who would know and care nothing about the things that occupy my thoughts? Should we not always remain strangers to each other, though nominally man and wife? Besides, should I not have rivals—jealous hating rivals! —sharing with me his time and his affections?"

Then Selim Mustapha turned upon his daughter a look of savage fierce mistrust, and he angrily exclaimed:

"Are you, then, going to turn traitress, Azzahra? What mean you by thus reviling the men of your own race and religion, by thus casting contempt on the social institutions of our fathers, established by the Holy Prophet himself? Are you going to take to yourself a lover from amongst the Christians? Tear such a thought from your breast, Azzahra, and fling it away! Never would I consent to such an unholy marriage—never would I submit to such degradation! Sooner would I behold you mouldering in your grave, slain by this right hand!"

Flinging herself on his neck, she replied in a passionate outburst of tears, for she was alarmed by these fiery denunciations:

"Oh! how can you suspect me of harbouring such thoughts? Believe me, my dear father, I care not for marriage at all—still less for a marriage of which you would not approve. Far, far sooner would I remain as I am, always with you to give you my undivided love! Nevertheless, your word shall ever be law unto me; deal with me even as you will."

"And is this your sole reason for not desiring marriage," he asked, with a keen scrutinising look—"the desire to be with your father?"

"It is, in truth, my sole reason, my father," replied the girl, colouring deeply at the deception she was practising; "I want no more than to be beside you."

"May Allah bless and keep you then, my daughter!" the fond father answered in softened tones. "Well I knew your good sense would prevail, guiding you in the paths of prudence and in dutiful submission to your parent."

"I must leave you now," he resumed, after embracing her, "to throw off this foul attire, and prepare myself to meet the rest of my household. But, mind, keep your counsel. Not a word to mortal that you have seen me in this disguise. Were it once known by the Bureau Arabe that I assume this dress, and were I tracked, in consequence of the discovery, among our tribes of the desert, after I leave for the South, my life might pay the forfeit, and so might the lives of my followers."

Azzahra had made a terrible self-sacrifice when she surrendered herself without reserve to her father's will; but, in her unbounded joy at having to accompany him far away, she weighed not the calamities such a vow of obedience might entail. Given in a moment of affectionate dutiful devotion, she meant her promise to be binding.

She foresaw not how little that vow would avail in the hour of trial, nor how soon it was going to be ruthlessly broken.

CHAPTER VI.

THE FOUNTAINS OF THE DJINS.

WHEN Selim Mustapha departed from his daughter's presence she clapped her little hands to summon her attendant, who had retired on recognising her master's voice, and the impetuous enthusiastic girl bounded forward to meet the Negress.

"Kredoudja!" she exclaimed in triumph. "What joy! We are to start at once for the Desert with my father. My prison-bars are to be opened at last, and I am to be free!"

To her surprise, the serving-girl, instead of rejoicing with her, as she expected, looked sad and thoughtful. After long silent reflection the Negress said:

"My dear mistress, have you well considered the risks you must encounter, the dangers you will have to brave?"

Looking round, to see they were alone, she added, whispering cautiously in Azzahra's ear:

"Have you not heard that Selim Mustapha is

suspected of being in communication with the
revolted tribes in the Desert, who cause such
anxiety and dismay to the Christians ?—in fact,
that many suspect him to be Si Sala, their leader ?
Do you know your father is an outlaw ?—that he
is under the close supervision of the Government? Have you not heard that a powerful
military expedition is even now being organized
in the west, to penetrate into the Sahara in
pursuit of these rebel bands? How would it
fare, then, with you amid such dangers ! "

"For me danger has no terrors," haughtily
replied Azzahra, not seeming to heed Kredoudja's allusion to her father's disloyalty, which
she strongly suspected was not devoid of foundation; though, after the caution he had given her,
she dared not open her mind even to the Black,
whom she ordinarily trusted in all things with
implicit confidence.

"But if you shrink from the prospect of
danger, come not along with me, Kredoudja,"
she went on. "Far wiser will it be to remain
here behind than to share with your mistress the
hardships of tent-life amongst the Children of
the Desert. It will be easy to procure some one
with more spirit and fidelity to accompany me
on my way."

She would not have spoken thus harshly, but
that she was mortified at what she unthinkingly
regarded as cold heartless apostasy on the part

of her waiting-woman. These heedless words gave a cruel blow to the devoted Soudanese, making her burst into a passionate flood of bitter tears.

"Allah knows," she sobbed, "it is not my own welfare, it is yours, I am considering! Oh, think, is it right, is it modest, for a young woman to place herself, as you propose, in the power of the savage hordes that wander through those lone regions, bound by no feelings of moral rectitude, acknowledging no legal obligation?"

"My father will protect me," retorted the wayward girl haughtily. "Who will dare harm me while he is near?"

"But he may not always be near," Kredoudja meekly replied. "He may perchance be forced to leave you in charge of his ruffian followers while absent on some distant expedition; then will come your hour of trial and peril."

With earnest entreaties she besought her mistress not to embark rashly and without due consideration in an enterprise that seemed so fraught with danger. She implored her, before making her final decision, to consult the Djins at the Ayoun-Beni- Menad near St. Eugène, in order to ascertain from this infallible source of truth whether the undertaking would be attended with favourable results.

For some time Azzahra pondered before giving a reply.

"I have been taught to believe not in the power of Evil Spirits," she said at length, though in tones that Kredoudja could perceive implied doubt as to the convictions she expressed. "Surely such beings do not exist."

"They do exist," said Kredoudja with confidence. "Oh! I entreat of you, my dear lady, not to form any resolution before taking this sure means for divining the future."

So urgent was the devoted attendant in her entreaties that Azzahra at length consented, though with reluctance, and promised Kredoudja that, for her sake, she would ask counsel of the Genii.

"To-morrow," said she to her delighted attendant, "we will repair to the Fountains of St. Eugène."

"Praise be to Allah!" exclaimed the Negress, overjoyed at her mistress's promise. "Even now I go to procure the victims for sacrifice."

As she was departing on this errand Azzahra called her back, for she sincerely loved her at heart.

"Forgive the way I spoke, Kredoudja," she exclaimed with warmth, to the profound joy of the Black. "I know I wronged you cruelly; I know that in what you advised you thought only of my good."

Delighted at heart by these soothing words

from her mistress, Kredoudja sped on her mission.

At early morn the two young women issued forth on their way to St. Eugène. Azzahra was wrapped in her white burnous, and her face was concealed by her haïk, all save her bright black sparkling eyes; while Kredoudja wore the blue striped burnous of her race, allowing her large massive features to remain uncovered. In her hand she carried by their tied-up legs the fluttering live fowls intended for sacrifice to the Djins.

Leaving Algiers by the Bab-el-Oued Gate, they passed through the French lines of circumvallation outside the town, and proceeded along the shore of the sea by the village of St. Eugène.

There they were constrained to pause on the road which runs parallel to the sea-wall, while a great seine-net was being drawn in to shore; for the fisherman hauling at the ropes occupied the entire width of the roadway, so as to bar all passage.

Azzahra was much surprised at the quantities of sardines and other small fish with which the coast abounds that were hauled in by the net, but which she had never seen before. How surprised would she have been to watch the fleet of five hundred vessels at Concarneau, on the Bay of Biscay, standing out to sea to fish for these little sardines, that seemed to her so insignificant as scarce to be worth the trouble of catching !

As soon as the road lay clear of the obstruction, they continued their course, and shortly arrived at the small cabaret along the road to the Pointe Pescade, where stood of old the Koubba (or Marabout) of Sidi-Yakoub, a saint who was in great favour with the Algerine Mahometan ladies, although fortunate in possessing at the same time a high reputation for unimpeachable sanctity and purity, which prevented husbands and fathers from becoming jealous of his frequent visits to their female relations. At this spot Azzahra and her attendant descended a slippery stony path that led down to a little inlet of the sea shut in by projecting rocks and cliffs, where a large concourse of fair worshippers were already gathered together to honour and consult the Genii of the Fountains.

When the two girls had clambered down the steep bank, they passed seven small bubbling rills that burst out of the hillside and trickled down over the shingle into the sea below. These were the Ayoun-Beni-Menad, or sacred Fountains of the Genii, each haunted by the particular Djin to whose worship it was specially dedicated.

Azzahra paused to learn from the Negress which springs were frequented by the evil Djins, and which by the good. Three of the springs

Kredoudja pointed out as the abodes of the good spirits—the White, the Blue, and the Green. The remaining four she told her mistress were haunted by the Red, the Yellow, the Brown, and the Black, who were the evil Djins.

As they stepped upon the beach Azzahra anxiously inquired whether they were about to sacrifice to the good or to the bad Djins, for she felt shocked at offering worship and sacrifice to an evil spirit.

"To both," replied the Soudanese; "but first we will sacrifice to the bad Genii, because they are the most powerful and the most to be feared. Should they prove friendly and smile on our enterprise we need be under no alarm as to what the others can do to us; afterwards it will be easy to invoke the aid of the good Djins, but in the first instance they are not worth the trouble of killing victims for, until we know what is going to happen!"

This arrangement astonished Azzahra, and somewhat outraged her religious feelings; but she concealed her scruples, following implicitly the instructions she received.

Azzahra now surveyed with curiosity and deep interest the striking scene before her.

On a small insulated reef of black rocks, separated by only a few feet of shallow water from the shore, sat a group of Negro musicians, who played on a sort of flageolet, beat drums, and kept up a loud dismal waiting vocal chant. This discordant uproar her guide informed Azzahra was made to attract the attention of the Genii to the ceremonies going forward in their honour.

Facing these lugubrious performers were ranged a row of officiating Moorish and Black priestesses, surrounded by worshippers who held victims ready in their hands for being offered in sacrifice. Before each priestess a brasier stood on the ground filled with burning coals, at which the incense in a censer she held in her hand was lighted.

Azzahra was greatly struck by the strange scene, and the weird old-world superstition and idolatry she saw before her—the bold black ledge of rocks washed by the waters of the sea, the wild overhanging cliffs, the doleful musicians, the Black and Moorish priestesses, and the crowd of eager worshippers waiting on the sands in anxious expectation for their turn to arrive, when they should be able to interrogate the Djins and learn their fate.

In olden times these mysterious rites were confined to the Soudanese population of Algiers that arrived as slaves from the far South of the Sahara and even from the centre of the African Continent, forming an important part of their heathenish religion.

But the desire of reading the future has possessed in all ages a magic charm and fascination for the human mind. Thus it has come to pass, that this means of consulting the Book of Fate through the local genii of the Ayoun-Beni-Menad has taken deep root among the illiterate Moorish, Jewish, and Arab women of Algiers. They acknowledge not the pagan religion of the Blacks, it is true, but they regard this gross superstition as an addendum to their respective faiths—a supplementary act of devotion, a sort of spiritual *hors d'œuvre*, which can do no harm and may do good. Though often belonging to the better classes, these fair devotees are as blind and as easily duped as the humblest British maidservant who hands over her hard-earned savings to the merciless clutches of the gipsy fortune-teller.

And can we wonder at silly women like these uncultivated Algerines, who know nothing of the world, being led away captive by such vain imaginations, when we remember what powerful intellects have been enslaved by similar gross superstitions ?

We know that amongst the nations of antiquity no important step in life was undertaken without previously asking counsel of soothsayers, augurs, and astrologers, and we know that Eastern nations still cling to the same barbarous custom. We know that Catherine de Medicis and, it is said, even the Great Napoleon were guilty of this unholy weakness, and sought to

read the events of the future by these forbidden
means.

The better class of African women come,
doubtless, to the Fountains more in a spirit of
curiosity than in a spirit of faith. They scarcely
believe that the spirits whom they thus igno-
rantly worship possess absolute control over
their lives or future prospects, as do the Soudanese. The ceremony is to them a species of
experimental philosophy—something that may
give great pleasure and comfort should it take a
favourable turn ; although, were the decision of
the Genii hostile to their wishes, the result would
not inflict any grievous amount of sorrow or
fear.

This is the same feeling with which foolish
girls of an humble position of life in our own
country betake themselves to the gipsy diviner
of the future. When the crafty Bohemian tells
them what they want to hear they depart contented, thinking they have received ample value
for the money extracted ; but when the revela-
tion is adverse, they set down the seer as either
ignorant or mistaken or malevolent, but never
do they acquiesce in the unfavourable sentence.

Was woman's heart ever broken because a
dark man had been prognosticated for her by
the pretended reader of futurity, instead of the
fair-haired lover of her choice ? Was woman's
mind ever driven to despair at not being told

she would have unbounded wealth at her command, or that she was destined to sweep past wondering duchesses and princesses in her coach-and-six? Will she not rather seek out another soothsayer, who will read her destiny more in accordance with what she considers the truth, and will tell her pleasant things such as she longs to hear?

But these scheming impostors seldom disappoint their victims, almost invariably laying themselves out to please. They know and look after their own interest too well, as a rule, to tell a bad "fortune" to their votaries.

It was in a doubting mood like this that Azzahra approached the mystic scene. Her education was too advanced—she had read too much—her mind was too cultivated to place reliance in these dealings with the supernatural, and she more than suspected that Djins were after all but unsubstantial creatures of the imagination. That such beings, even should they actually exist, could exercise material control over the destinies of man she scouted as a monstrous absurdity—when she reasoned; but she did not always reason.

And do not we on occasion try to banish reasoning from our minds? Have we no perplexing matters we tacitly accept as truths which in our heart of hearts we regard with lurking suspicion—about which we desire not

to reason, not even to think? Have we besides no matters we earnestly wish to believe,
but from which reason obstinately persists in
recoiling?

Relinquishing thus the exercise of her judgment, Azzahra surrendered herself to the direction of the Negress, who gave undoubting
credence to the omnipotence and omniscience
of the Djins. Independently of Kredoudja's
arguments and assertions, other considerations
tended to shake and unsteady her mind. Those
of her own flesh and blood, by reason of their
want of culture, she held but in low repute, yet
she could not conceal from herself the fact that
every inmate of her father's house warmly con-
curred with the Black in entertaining the highest
veneration for these superstitious observances.
In spite of herself this consideration strongly
influenced her at times. The gentle unsophisticated child of Nature often felt timorous at
setting up her private judgment against her
elders with their longer experience of life, and
consequently with their greater knowledge of
the world, narrow-minded and illiterate though
she knew them to be.

At times indeed, in her maidenly humility,
she almost felt it a duty to conform to their
opinions, and to sacrifice, in deference to them,
her own doubting scruples.

But her mind had been developed by education

too much to permit such an absolute abnegation and surrender of her convictions; and so she drifted on, like too many others in the world, doubting, though reluctant to own her doubts.

Thus it was that she approached the Ayoun-Beni-Menad and gave herself over to the worship of the Djins, entertaining no tangible, clearly defined belief in the mystic rites, yet unwilling to pronounce them an imposture. She joined in the sacred ceremonies neither in the spirit of a blind bigoted devotee nor of a confirmed unbeliever.

The course of action she marked out proved this, for even in the event of the spirits being unpropitious she determined still to accompany her father to the Sahara, her restless spirit yearning after wild exciting adventures.

"I burn to become a Child of the Desert," she exclaimed, as her cheek warmed and her eye flashed.

On the other hand, should favourable omens be vouchsafed, she knew what comfort and confidence they would afford to her simple trusting waiting-maid; and the suspicion began to creep into her mind that, although still incredulous, she might set forth herself with a lighter heart.

"If Djins exist not I have done no harm in coming here," she argued. "If there are such beings it is well to propitiate them and secure their favour."

In either case therefore there could be no risk incurred; on the contrary, she would be adopting the safest and wisest course.

How many among us think in this spirit of their religious faith!—how many die in this spirit! At the last, after a life of neglect, often of hostility, towards the religion they profess, they tremblingly crave her consolations, as a possible though improbable chance in their favour in the world to come.

So, her mind filled with these quibbling, doubting, wavering sentiments, Azzahra tripped lightly along, conducted by Kredoudja, to where an obese unveiled Moorish priestess stood upon the shelving strand, close to the black rocks whence the discordant sounds of the musicians proceeded. This priestess was a special favourite, wherefore some time transpired before Azzahra's turn came round to claim her ministrations.

When the woman beckoned to her to advance, Kredoudja untied the group of struggling and shrieking fowls, selecting one as an offering.

This bird the priestess carried to the fountain of the evil spirit to whom it was about to be sacrificed, where she sprinkled its feathers with the sacred water. She then handed the dripping fowl together with a large sharp knife to Azzahra, desiring her to take it in her hands and cut its throat with the knife. But the timid novice shrank from such a deed of blood, which Kredoudja at once volunteered without scruple to perform on her behalf.

However, this was not permitted, for the Mauresque declared that she alone, as priestess, was competent to act in lieu of worshippers who objected to slay their own victims, because were the rite performed by a third person the Genii would not hearken, and the sacrifice would be null and void.

The priestess therefore took the fowl from the hands of Kredoudja, and carried it from the spring to the top of the sloping beach of shingle that shelved down to the Mediterranean. There she ran the knife across its throat, and, flinging it down, left it to struggle on the ground. Long it fluttered, giving convulsive jumps in its dying agonies without moving away from the spot where it had fallen, to the intense dismay of Kredoudja and the Mauresque priestess, who explained to Azzahra that this was an unfavourable omen, for the dying bird would have rolled down the incline into the sea were the Djin propitious to whom it had been presented.

At length, after all hope of a successful issue had been nearly abandoned, and the suppliants were concluding that they were under the baneful displeasure of the Djin, the fowl gave a last expiring bound into the air, rolling over and

over down to the foot of the pebbly slope, where
it miserably perished in the waters.

Joy now beamed from every countenance,
the Mauresque complimenting Azzahra on the
happy termination of the ceremony, while she
tore out the reeking entrails from the body of
the chicken and flung them into the sea.

In like manner the remaining malevolent
spirits were inquired of, all of whom gave undoubted evidence of cordiality, the unhappy
chickens precipitating themselves into the waves
in a most orderly and satisfactory manner.

Fowls were afterwards offered with similar
ceremony to the benevolent Genii, two of whom
manifested decidedly refractory tendencies; for
their chickens refused obstinately to stir from
where they were thrown down, and breathed
their last in obstinate contumacy.

At this result Azzahra felt mortified, though
scarcely owning such a feeling to herself; and
Kredoudja was likewise much depressed in
spirit, as on such an occasion she wished for an
unanimous verdict, although she had always
heard that this was not by any means an indis-
pensable requisite. However, the Moorish
priestess assured them they might rest satisfied
with the results obtained, and might reckon on
the favouring aid of both good and evil spirits in
whatever matter they wished to undertake.

"It only remains for you now," she added,

addressing Azzahra, " to receive the final rites."
She then lighted the incense in her brazen
censer at the chafing-dish before her, at the
same time opening the burnous and haïk of her
votary. Making Azzahra lean on her shoulder,
she knelt down and lifted up the girl's feet
divested of slippers, which she held for a few
seconds over the smoke of the aromatic com-
pound. Both sides of the hands were similarly
fumigated, and so was the head. The Mauresque pushed up her censer beneath Azzahra's
haïk, which required to be lifted for the purpose,
so that the bright-blue zouave trousers beneath,
embroidered in gold lace, could be distinctly
seen by the black musicians opposite upon the
rocks, who still kept up their droning dismal wail.

Azzahra imagined that none of the other sex
save these Negroes, whose presence seemed
to be unheeded, had enjoyed the privilege of
beholding her symmetrical form. But she was
mistaken. Another there was on the bank
above who watched every movement, and
whose heart became deeply impressed with the
beauty and gracefulness of the fair devotee's
youthful slender figure, thus unwittingly revealed to his admiring gaze.

A like fumigation at the back, which could
not be distinctly observed from aloft, owing to
the burnous concealing so much from view,
completed the mystic ceremony.

By this process the suppliant was purified, so as to be duly qualified for asking what she would of the Genii with a certainty that her prayer would be granted.

Azzahra made the Mauresque priestess a handsome present, and was proceeding to re-ascend the steep path up the hill, delighted with the auspicious result of her expedition, when the Negress entreated her to remain until the dead fowls had been picked up, some from off the beach, some out of the water.

On arriving again at the Ayoun-Beni-Menad, Azzahra addressed a short prayer to the Genii, under the direction of Kredoudja, imploring their assistance and protection in her projected journey.

She well knew that an audible response to her prayers would not be returned, still she could not refrain from a vague feeling of disappoint-ment that no voice came to comfort and soothe, to give assurance of her petition being granted. In her studies she had read of the oracles of antiquity where immediate answers were vouch-safed to the inquiries of votaries, and she de-plored that such a practical mode of reading the future should not still be in existence. How many, she thought, would pray then who pray not now! How much stronger would be the hold of religion on mankind were it felt to be a positive certainty that prayer would be heard and answered!

Had Azzahra seen the ruins of the old Roman Temple of Diana at Nimes she would have understood the gross deception practised at these shrines of old. She would have seen the chimney-like aperture behind the high altar, down which the priest or priestess descended from the dwellings of the clergy above to personate the goddess and reply in her name to the faithful.

As soon as her devotions were concluded, Azzahra asked her attendant for what use she intended the dead fowls she was going to collect.

"Surely none would eat these wretched draggled objects," she asked, "after they have been offered in sacrifice?"

"They are none the worse for that," replied Kredoudja, stuffing them into a basket she carried for the purpose. "Look round, and you will see that not one is left behind."

"So I perceive," continued her mistress in astonishment. "But what are those common, meanly dressed French women gathering off the shingle and washing in the sea?"

"Those are the entrails of the victims," answered the other, "which you noticed the priestess threw away when preparing the birds for sacrifice."

"And is it possible that our conquerors can feed on such revolting garbage, which I should hesitate to throw to a dog?" exclaimed Azzahra, deeply disgusted.

"These people are miserably poor," the Black replied, shrugging her shoulders, "and are thankful to pick up eatables in any shape. Even this offal, the sight of which offends you, is a perfect godsend to the struggling wretches, who are the dregs and offscourings of the European population."

"I should have thought a Christian would perish from starvation sooner than partake of sacrifices offered to evil spirits," Azzahra went on, "for I know they are taught in their Great Book to abstain from such food."

"Our masters seem to pay but little heed to their Great Book, or to the precepts their priests inculcate," the Soudanese continued. "They appear to think their sole duties are to conquer and oppress—to kill, plunder, and destroy."

By this time the two young women had remounted the hill. Following a sharp turning in the path as she reached the summit, Azzahra stepped out upon the highroad, when she found herself face to face with Wilton. Her heart beat high as she approached, for she at once remembered the scene in the Marengo Gardens, and the glowing admiration which he had then inspired. That he was of a different race and a different creed she well knew, but such unromantic considerations, in her ardent enthusiasm, she heeded not. She felt intuitively he was one, whoever and whatever he might be, to whom she could look up with worshipping homage, and whom she could love to distraction. The sweet smile that lighted up his fine fresh features, his tall lithe manly figure, his noble appearance, completely enthralled her and took possession of her heart, as now she looked on him once again; so that, casting away all dictates of wisdom, oblivious of country, of religion, and even of her father's ire, she thought she could live beside him for ever, and be happy even as his slave.

When once the wild storm of passion sweeps through the breast, and the God of Love takes his seat on the throne of the heart, what does the victim of his shafts care for cold calculating reflections about prudence or duty? Frenzied ecstasy and yearning greed for possession of the loved object hold paramount sway, to the contemptuous exclusion of every conflicting consideration; conscience and prudence are ignominiously scouted as troublesome unwelcome intruders.

As Azzahra drew near to Wilton their eyes met, when the electric thrill of passionate emotion flashed wildly afresh through her throbbing, burning Southern veins with tenfold intensity.

In an instant she was transformed. Her life—her woman's life—had begun. A few seconds before she was a child; now she felt the glorious intoxicating power of womanhood. She felt she was a child no longer, and had for ever put away childish things. Her pulse was madly beating—her head was swimming. She was a helpless victim to love, of which she had so often heard and dreamed, but whose power she had never known before.

While passing Wilton her veil fell from before her face, so that her lovely features were revealed to his delighted gaze. Did this occur designedly or by accident? By accident Wilton implicitly believed.

Blushing deeply she hastened to conceal her features again, but not before Henry had ample time to survey their exceeding loveliness. The perfect symmetry of her form he had gazed on before and ardently admired, while she stood below before the Mauresque priestess with her burnous lifted to one side, though she believed no man had enjoyed that privilege save the black musicians on the rocks.

Deeply was he smitten by the surpassing beauty of her face as he looked while she went by, and this her ready woman's instinct led her to perceive—a conviction that sent renewed thrills of rapture through her frame, awakening feelings that had hitherto lain dormant within.

She cherished the hope that Wilton would

accost her on the plea of offering some remark concerning the ceremonies he had watched with such interest.   What more natural or more plausible excuse could offer, she thought, for forming her acquaintance?

And a strong inclination had tempted him to address her, entranced as he was by admiration of her wondrous beauty. After having passed her, even, he was on the point of turning to overtake her. But the cherished image of Olinda rose up before him; the disloyalty of permitting another, even for a moment, to take her place brought the colour to his cheek: he hesitated, and the opportunity was lost. So she slowly moved away—sadly, very sadly—for she would have given worlds, did she possess them, to hold sweet communion with the captivating stranger. But, alas! it was not to be, and she walked on, silently and sorrowfully, wrapt in mournful reflections.

Kredoudja had taken notice of all. She saw her young mistress unveil, which she shrewdly suspected had not happened unintentionally, though Azzahra subsequently professed to regard the occurrence with shame and confusion. Perhaps the serving-girl thought of the proverb, " *Qui s'excuse s'accuse,*" but she prudently kept her counsel, freely offering condolence at such an untoward event.

Azzahra's little fluttering heart was too full,

however, to keep silence long before her chosen confidante. Soon she commenced to open her mind, and to enlarge enthusiastically on the perfections of Wilton, to the profound astonishment and dismay of the Soudanese, who remembered in what impassioned strains her mistress had praised him before in the Marengo Gardens.

"Such thoughts you must banish, my dear lady," the Negress exclaimed in affright, on hearing Azzahra's confession. "You know full well the deadly hatred in which your father holds the Franks."

"But he is not French, Kredoudja, believe me," the weeping girl pleaded. "That soft gentle sweet expression of countenance is not such as our conquerors possess. He has not their insolent defiant manner as they clatter their swords at their heels, nor has he their dissipated appearance. Did I believe him one of the enemies of my country, I would tear his image from my heart, however dearly I might love him!"

"Of that I am convinced," replied the Black, though after a little hesitation. "You need never hope, however, to take for a husband a dweller in Europe, no matter to what nation he may belong. The Infidels are an abomination in the sight of Selim Mustapha. Put away, then, this senseless caprice from your thoughts, otherwise untold misery must follow.   Besides, remember, we may be summoned at any moment to depart for the lands of the South; then what would become of your love adventure, when you could see your lover no more?"

The force of this reasoning could not be gain-said.   Whatever unhappiness might ensue, Az-zahra owned, with a deep sigh, it was now too late to draw back from her promise to her father. Go she must, at all hazards.

"Of course you must go," gladly joined in Kredoudja.   "After the Djins having been so propitious, it would be downright wickedness and madness to fly in their faces by refusing to comply with their wishes, so clearly expressed."

Azzahra did not feel quite certain on this point, but she assented without comment.

"Yes, it would be unwise to stay, I own," she answered in sorrow.   "But that European I never shall, I never can, forget.   Firmly am I persuaded, Kredoudja, that he and I are destined to meet again."

CHAPTER VII.

A DISCOVERY.

WHEN Henry Wilton next visited at the Villa Isly, he found Olinda engaged in arranging a showy spirited set of waltzes for the pianoforte, which she had recently composed. She played them for him with the artistic feeling and earnestness of successful genius, and when she had finished her large lustrous blue eyes glanced upwards, as though demanding applause. Wilton cordially admired the graceful compositions, and gladly bestowed on her a liberal award of praise.

But while pouring lavish compliments into her willing ear, he could not suppress a sigh at the transparent exultation which she displayed, and at the greedy avidity with which she drank in his glaring flattery. The sorrow he had of late experienced came back with redoubled force. This deplorable tendency to court and invite compliments he had often noticed, and he felt deeply grieved to think that such a brilliant

lovable disposition should be so fatally marred
by this one sad blemish—this one little speck
upon the luscious fruit—this one little canker in
the blooming flower—this one little rift in the
tuneful lute—this one little flaw in the beauteous work of art. Would the speck turn to
decay? he thought. Would the canker destroy
and annihilate? Would the rift hush the melodious sounds? Would the flaw spread, so as
to rend in pieces the fair artistic composition?

Alas! he knew woman's weakness, and trembled. He shuddered to reflect what an easy
prey his fair cousin would be in the hands of a
clever silver-tongued base intriguer, who would
gratify *ad nauseam* this appetite for adulation,
and who would dazzle her at the same time with
his own tinsel counterfeit merits.

He thought of the Marquis de St. Bertrand
again, with his polished winning manners and
his hollow heart.

How lamentable, he reflected once more, that
one so far exalted above ordinary women in
intellect and soul—so pure, so chaste, so good,
so angelic, so adorable—should nevertheless
place herself, in this single instance, on a level
with the lightest and weakest and most frivolous
of her sex!

His love for Olinda—love he believed to burn
as brightly as ever—made him hope that she
might never fall into the snares of a man like

this; for well he knew the result to her proud
spirit would be eternal misery, united to one
who had deceived and entrapped her.

Of late these saddening thoughts flashed often
with vivid force through his mind, when Olinda
would pointedly display in his presence consciousness of mental superiority to himself,
filling him with deep pain and sorrow, for her
sake more than for his—thoughts he had never
harboured of old.   But this day the compas-
sionate sadness wherewith he witnessed her
unconcealed insensate gratification at his in-
ordinate encomiums on her talents—which, to
test her, he had purposely made in the highest
degree fulsome—struck deeper and more intensely than ever.

Why this new and unfavouring criticism of his
cousin, who he hitherto thought could do no
wrong? The reason he could not divine. He
was unconscious as yet that the iron had entered
into his soul when his eyes met the soft gentle
bewitching glances of Azzahra, when he drank
in the modest beauties of her blushing unveiled
charms. He was unconscious that his admiration had already begotten love. He was unconscious that comparisons—invidious comparisons
—were already surging through his mind; that
he was already contrasting, unfavourably to his
cousin, her studied selfish coldness whenever he
tried to touch her heart, as compared with the

sweet feminine innocent appearance of the
Arab maiden. Of all this he was unconscious,
because he still firmly believed in his great,
unalterable, undying devotion for Olinda.

But he knew not himself. He knew not that
his feelings towards Olinda were simply those of
esteem and of admiration—worship it might be—
for her glorious intellect, but not those of intense
unfading love. Her diagnosis of him was just,
when she told him he loved her not deeply, and
would soon learn to forget. With the true
sagacity of woman she had read him aright.

A less ethereal temperament—more bending,
more genial, more feminine—was what Henry
needed to win his sympathy, and inspire a pure
earnest devoted flame within his breast—a
flame that would endure for ever. His was a
warm trusting disposition, that sighed for
gentleness and reciprocity—almost, indeed, for
support.

Fate, however, with its usual persistent cruelty,
had hitherto denied him those inestimable boons.
At Olinda's hands he looked for them in vain.

After so long a time he began to suspect at
last that he had made a grave blunder in placing
his affections upon one so completely wrapped
up in self and in her little learned circle. Grand
and beautiful though he owned her to be, he
owned also that a tender feeling would assuredly
never have taken possession of his heart but for

the accidental circumstance that the two held such constant intercourse together by reason of his oft-repeated visits.

The old proverb that "familiarity breeds contempt" is unquestionably true, but it is equally true that familiarity between man and woman has a powerful tendency to breed the soft sentiments of love.

But love was not the sole attracting influence that drew Henry towards Olinda. He thought she would show kindness and affection to his fondly loved sister; he thought she would be domestic, and would make him domestic as well; he thought she would be leal and true.

Such were his motives—such the considerations that perverted his judgment, and forced him into the belief that he was slave to a passion he never truly experienced. The veil, however, was soon to be lifted up from before his sight, when he was no longer to see through a glass darkly, but face to face. And the process of disenchantment —the knowledge of his altered sensations— broke upon him suddenly and sharply.

He was narrating to Olinda, who listened with deep curiosity and interest, the extraordinary scene of pagan old-world worship he had witnessed at the Ayoun-Beni-Menad. He told her of the horrid din made by the black musicians, the slaughter and the dying struggles of the victims offered in sacrifice to the Genii, the invocations and ceremonials of the officiating priestesses, the profound devotion of the worshippers, the unreserved freedom with which young girls as well as grown-up women allowed their faces to remain unveiled and their under-costumes to be revealed during the celebration of these strange mysterious rites, and likewise the disgusting behaviour of the French hangers-on in collecting the foul refuse to be devoured as human food.

"But surely none except the lowest scum of the natives took part in those heathenish ceremonies?" Olinda exclaimed interrogatively, when he had concluded his recital, shocked and disgusted at what she heard of the degrading scene.

"Pardon me," Wilton interrupted in a tone of impatience, "several native ladies attended there, to consult the Genii. One Moorish lady drove there in her carriage, accompanied by two female attendants of her own race, and likewise by a Negress, who carried in her hand the sacrificial victims. There was also a young girl present I judged by her features to be an Arab, one of the most perfect beings I ever laid eyes on. Do you remember, Olinda, the native, accompanied by a Soudanese attendant, whom you told me to look at and admire in the Jardin Marengo, and whom Geraldine laughingly said she overheard talking about me? I positively believe this young Arab girl to be the very same, and you would have admired her ten times more than you did that day had you seen the soft and guileless yet intellectual expression of her lovely face."

"How came you to see her unveiled?" said Olinda, looking at him in surprise. "The native women remain closely veiled in the presence of strange men—at least those who care for their reputation."

For the first time Henry could realise what was passing within. For the moment he felt guilty before Olinda. He felt the change that had come over him. He felt as though he had betrayed her in thought, though not in word or deed. He was so conscience-stricken and abashed that he scarce knew how to reply. But this weakness was not for long. At once he reasserted his independence, shaking off the spell by which she had hitherto enslaved him. He became transformed into a new man, and put away his misplaced humility.

By what right, he asked himself, did Olinda undertake to question him, or pry into his affairs? Why should she seek to know what passed between himself and this Arab? Why should she constitute herself a ruler and a judge over him? He had offered her his heart, and she had spurned him as intellectually unworthy. He denied then her claim to inquire into what concerned him, unmindful, in his unreasoning excitement, of the mutual intimacy and affection that had always existed between them. He felt almost disposed to resent her interference, still more her implied censure on Azzahra's behaviour. The censure, he felt sure, was unmerited; he felt sure Azzahra was pure and modest, and the disparaging insinuation against her therefore sank deep into his heart.

Such was the sudden powerful revulsion of feeling created by his cousin's comments on what Azzahra had done. The significance of this act of the lovely Arab had not struck him before in its true light. Hitherto he had attributed the circumstance to chance, and had compassionated her for what he supposed must have caused deep shame and pain at the time. Now he began to surmise there was foundation for Olinda's suspicion that the unveiling was not accidental, that to confer on him a special mark of favour Azzahra had departed purposely from the customs of her people, and that she had conformed for his sake to the customs of Europe.

That the act had been dictated by immodest or unmaidenly forwardness, as his cousin would have him suppose, he indignantly repudiated. He became persuaded that, done in all purity, it was prompted solely by love—love for him, seeking to win his love in return; for that she was the same whom Geraldine heard in the Marengo Gardens eulogise him so warmly he felt convinced. She could not have failed to observe him gazing on her from the cliffs at the Fountains of the Genii, he argued, and doubtless the discovery confirmed the belief Geraldine heard her express that she had found favour in his sight. How natural, then, the desire on her part to prove that she reciprocated his tender passion!

Convinced by these soothing love-inspiring considerations, he thought of her with far more exceeding fondness, and bewailed his want of gallantry in neglecting the opportunity she gave him to address her.

Her foreign birth, her supposed want of refined education, her participation even in heathenish rites, all vanished out of sight, like mists of the morning, when he thought of the tender glance, the winning smile, the intellectual look, the noble bearing of the beautiful dark-eyed houri at whose feet he fain would kneel and worship.

Olinda's inquiring curiosity had been the means of removing the scales from his eyes so that he could see clearly, and he had entered upon a new life. Truly has it been said—

"Behold how great a flame a little fire kindleth!"

A wondrous change had in truth been wrought. Far from feeling now that he was wronging Olinda by suffering his thoughts to wander towards another, he advocated Azzahra's cause, arguing that his cousin had grievously wronged her by casting against her such opprobrious insinuations. That he loved his fair incognita he had discovered, but as yet he thought not of laying down any decided course of action for the future. He yearned after her and longed to call her his own. That was all he knew, all he cared for.

Mortified at Olinda's covert aspersions, he replied, with some asperity and in diametrical opposition to his inward convictions, that the young lady had evidently unveiled by accident.

Olinda had sufficient quickness of perception to take in at a glance how matters stood, but she prudently held her counsel, though confident that Wilton was concealing the truth, and that more had taken place than he allowed—in fact, that he cared already, perhaps passionately, for this fair heathen.

It piqued her that he should so soon have forgotten her for a rival—and such a rival! Still she had never thought of him seriously as a lover, nor allowed his advances; consequently the unwelcome discovery gave her no more than a slight pang. It did give her a pang though, for which she strove in vain to account, but which savoured strongly of jealousy, albeit she would not own this, even to herself. Against Azzahra she felt bitter and hostile, for she scouted the notion of the unveiling being unpremeditated. She thought that the fact of a girl brought up, like Azzahra, in seclusion from the other sex, according as her religion enjoined, uncovering before a perfect stranger was a convincing proof of reckless levity—nay, perhaps worse even, of designing treachery— and she sighed to think that Henry should become a prey to such transparent devices of an illiterate unbeliever.

"You style this pretty idolatress a lady, Henry?" she asked, with a strong dash of sarcasm and acrimony in her voice.

"She has every appearance of being a lady," Henry answered impatiently.

"I should have scarcely thought a lady would join in heathen mysteries," she went on. "I could understand persons in lowly life doing so, but not any one well brought up. In our country, for example, would any woman above a maid-servant or a milliner perpetrate so gross an outrage against common-sense as to seek through supernatural means to pry into futurity?"

"You scoff at maidservants and women of the same class in the humbler walks of life for giving credence to fortune-tellers and similar impostors," returned Wilton, regardless of Olinda's taunts, "implying that you think persons of higher position in life and of superior attainments incapable of being led away by foolish superstitions. But is this insinuation true,

Olinda? Have you never seen degraded grovelling superstition in our own rank of life? For
instance, have you never seen friends of yours
refuse to sit down thirteen to table? You know
you have. I have, lots of times—in the case too
of people one would little suspect of such preposterous credulity."

"It is too true," answered Olinda, "and I
have often found difficulty in restraining my
inclination to express the contempt such gross
folly inspires."

"How then about spiritualism and table-
rapping?" he asked, looking at her scruti-
nisingly, for he had heard of her attending
spiritualistic meetings. "Have you never been
to a *séance*?—only, of course, in a philosophical
spirit of inquiry."

"Indeed, I am ashamed to own my trans-
gressions," she replied, while a deep blush
betrayed her annoyance at the secret having
transpired. "However, it was solely from
curiosity I went, I assure you; I never for a
moment believed in the spirits."

"Oh, of course not!" he proceeded, a smile
slightly approaching to a sneer playing round
his lips. "And did you find the spirits com-
plaisant? Were they liberal in their manifesta-
tions?"

"Wondrously obliging," she replied, with
somewhat of cold dignity and bitterness, for her

cousin's mocking tone piqued her. "They swung guitars over our heads, rapped on the table, dragged chairs from beneath us, mounted chairs upon tables, pulled our hair and our noses, slapped our faces, and played sundry other fantastic tricks of a highly materialistic and unspiritual character."

"Of course you know how these tricks are done?" continued Henry, surveying her; "for that they are but conjuring tricks I suppose you will admit. You cannot lend yourself to believe that genuine spirits are in reality summoned for your entertainment from the vasty deep?"

"How could I believe in such absurdity?" she answered, looking confused and ashamed.

"Then can you form no idea of how the clever deceptions were practised?"

"I cannot imagine," she said, much perplexed. "Our hands were joined in a continuous chain round the table, and the door was locked before the lights were put out, so that none could enter the room. How these things occurred, therefore, is past comprehension."

"Nothing simpler," he observed, while the faintest tinge of exultation was perceptible in his voice. "You thought the hands of yourself and the others sitting round the table remained joined together the whole time, but you were deceived. The 'medium' contrived to join together the hands of those on either side of him in the dark so adroitly that both were unaware he had withdrawn his own. The moment this was done he was free to leave his seat, pass where he chose, strike the table to represent the rappings of the spirits, upset chairs, swing objects through the air past the heads of his dupes, and perform as many similar miracles as he wished, or as he thought the audience had patience to sit out. With a conspirator on either side of the 'medium,' who would let him break at will the chain and rise to move round the room, this could be arranged still more easily."

Wilton felt a slight sensation of illnatured triumph on seeing Olinda's palpable vexation at finding out by what transparent deceit the scheming spiritualists had befooled her, for he was beginning to take to heart the galling manner in which she had always inclined to presume on her learning and cleverness, notwithstanding her goodness of disposition. So he was not sorry to see her somewhat humbled, and forced to plead ignorance for once.

Yet he willingly made every allowance for her harmless waywardness. He pitied her for this unfortunate foible, her only blemish; and he trusted that, as she grew older and acquired more experience, her enthusiasm for talent-worship in herself and others would become gradually modified—perhaps even completely eradicated.

Meanwhile the chain which had so long bound him as a slave was broken. He was free, and she knew it. Her prophecy that he would soon forget his passion had received speedier fulfilment than even she anticipated. He had made the discovery that he could love another better than he loved her, and she now discovered, to her grief, by his altered manner that he had made this discovery.

She now felt that by her pride and loveless-ness she had placed a lump of ice next his heart, and that she had lost him for ever, whether for weal or for woe.

How true it is that, although, according to the old proverb, "Love begets love," the converse equally holds good—namely, that want of love begets want of love.

Too late this truth flashed across the mind of Olinda, and when Wilton departed she sought her chamber, and wept the bitter tears of repentance.

CHAPTER VIII.

WELCOME RECOGNITION.

WHILE Henry Wilton and some friends were conversing in the spacious court of the Hôtel de l'Orient, Mahmoud, the hotel guide, a descendant of the Turkish Corsairs, came to announce that a young Arab lad was about to be made a member of the Mahometan religion, and he offered to take any with him who desired to witness the religious ceremony.

The boy's father, the Turk stated, had once been a powerful Arab chieftain in the interior of Algeria, before the Government, doubtful of his fidelity, deprived him of his rank and compelled him to live in the city, where he could be kept under supervision and rendered powerless for carrying out the treasonable designs of which he was strongly suspected.

" But report says," added Mahmoud, confidentially, to the English present, "that he continues to elude the vigilance of our masters, stealing away for months at a time—whither none can tell."

Wilton was sad at heart—sad at having discovered how unreal and evanescent had been his devotion to Olinda—sad at losing Azzahra, most probably never to behold her more; for how could he hope to find her in the labyrinthine network of jealously guarded dwellings that compose the native quarter of the city?

With gladness therefore he hailed the opportunity of diverting the course of his thoughts into some fresh channel, and joined his compatriots in accompanying the Turk.

The party mounted the hill to the upper town by the tangled maze of steep narrow passages that wind up among the mysterious abodes of the natives—abodes which they had long but vainly desired to penetrate and examine.

At a large massive portal Mahmoud stopped and led them into the mansion of Selim Mustapha, where the ceremony they had come to see was to take place.

After they had gazed around in admiration at the luxurious abode—its rich marble courts, its groves of lemons and oranges, its gushing fountains, its brilliant array of many-coloured flowers, its richly sculptured walls, and all its attractive beauty—Mahmoud led the way, up a wide flight of marble stairs, to where the owner of the luxurious abode stood above, waiting to receive his guests, arrayed in rich attire, and having his fingers covered with enormous precious stones mounted in coarse silver setting, the manufacture of Kabyle jewellers.

A large concourse of friends, men swarthy and scowling like himself, surrounded him, with whom he engaged in earnest conversation. But when the strangers approached he came forward and put out his hand in European fashion to bid them welcome, politely expressing satisfaction at his good fortune in being enabled to let them see one of the most interesting ceremonials of his country and religion.

That a man of evident wealth and occupying a high position should admit strangers to partake of his hospitality on the invitation of a hotel dragoman struck Henry as remarkable.

"This entertainment has been given with a deep hidden purpose," whispered the Turk, whom Wilton had asked for an explanation of the mystery. "Is it likely, think you, that he would allow the privacy of his home to be interfered with by us to-day without some good reason? No—no! His motive is this. He hopes the French authorities may chance to hear of this fête, which will set their minds at rest about his being safe in their midst, when he may be even now, perchance, on the very eve of starting off, disguised, to the interior bent upon some desperate adventure."

A loud clattering here resounded through the halls of marble beneath and up the staircase, when a dashing young French officer, in a rich hussar uniform of crimson and dark-green, joined the group, his sword trailing and loudly clanking upon the ground as he carelessly lounged along. Henry at once recognised him as the Marquis de St. Bertrand, who had shown so much politeness at the Kasbah, and the two renewed their acquaintance with apparent cordiality.

The Marquis addressed Henry in excellent English, which he spoke with considerable fluency and with very little foreign accent, although at the Kasbah he had only employed his own language. This seemed so strange to Henry that he took an opportunity of good-humouredly expressing his surprise.

"It is our custom," answered the Marquis, shrugging his shoulders, and gaily adding: "We think it so amusing to hear you English committing yourselves and making such extraordinary remarks about us under the belief that we know nothing of what you are saying."

Wilton could not join in the hearty laugh of the hussar at conduct which appeared to him dishonourable and ungentlemanlike—unhandsome deception, in which he had previously detected our friends across the Channel.

"Here I am forced to converse with you in

your language," St. Bertrand continued, " because these *gamin* fellows all understand
French, and I do not want them to know what
you and I are speaking about. The fact is, the
Bureau Arabe have sent me here specially to
look after this old scoundrel Selim Mustapha,
one of the most deceitful treacherous rebels at
heart in the whole of Algeria, and who would
be one of the very first to rise against us to-
morrow did he but get the chance. But we
watch the vile traitor too closely to let him get
an opportunity for putting his black designs
into practice. Our spies are always round his
door, so that he cannot move even an inch from
home without our knowledge."

Wilton was much amused at this boast after
what Mahmoud had told him.

" The arch-rebel well knows I have come here
as a spy on him," continued the hussar. "He
knows well that I want not to look at any foul
rite or mystery of an accursed infidel faith. See
how he and his colleagues in villainy scowl at me
over there beneath their lowering brows, though
ready, if I commanded, to fling themselves on
the ground and lick the dust off my feet."

And rightly he estimated those men and the
significant glances that passed on the arrival of
the intruder. But the host advanced to welcome
with cringing humility the self-invited guest,
whom he meekly thanked in terms of abject

respect for honouring with his presence such an humble abode—fulsome homage listened to with cold haughty politeness, and only acknowledged by a slight inclination of the head.

In a patronising tone St. Bertrand then began to compliment Wilton on the loveliness of his cousin, and to tell what pleasure he felt in having made her acquaintance at the Kasbah, which gave such deep offence to the latter that he could with difficulty reply politely to the Frenchman.

"So you like not to hear the praises of the fair Olinda," muttered the hussar to himself. "You want to win her yourself, no doubt, and feel jealous; but, as I live, you shall not possess her; though I have to shoot you—you shall not! I love her, and she shall be mine! I swear it, come what may!"

And he moved on, while a black scowl crossed his knitted brows.

The moment the supercilious hussar had passed, the smooth oily impassive smile of the hot-blooded Arab vanished, giving place to a black malevolent look of rage that settled on his fine well-formed features; for his savage hatred of the Franks now burned with tenfold intensity, fanned into flame by the studied slights and insults offered by the intruding stranger in the presence of his relatives and friends.

"Aha! you come here to play the spy, do

you?" he muttered, grinding his teeth with impotent fury—"to trample, because you deem me humbled and fallen? But little you suspect you have blindly walked into the trap I laid to catch you. Little you suspect that while you go to report to your Bureau Arabe that the captive bird is safe in his cage, I shall be gone far hence, among the free of the Desert. Oh! would I might meet you there face to face, base spying coward that you are, and plunge deep this dagger into your false craven heart!"

But his duties as host demanded that he should master his furious passion, wherefore he smilingly conducted his guests along the balconied gallery, up whose trellis-covered sides creeping plants climbed in rich profusion from the court beneath, and on whose mosaic floor were tastefully ranged a profusion of choice flowers, in earthenware vessels of exquisite shapes and workmanship, manufactured by the natives in the mountain villages of Kabylia, to the eastward of Algiers, and in the Chenoua Mountains above Cherchel.

Entering a spacious apartment which opened on to the gallery, he sat down on the ground in Oriental fashion, with his feet crossed in front, and motioned to his guests to follow his example. The movement was easily performed by the Mahometans, who were accustomed to the posture, but it presented considerable difficulty to the Europeans, several of whom, including St. Bertrand, did not even try to accomplish the feat, merely sitting on the ground with their feet outstretched, or reclining on one elbow.

In the centre of the chamber stood a small square wooden framework on legs, with a large hollow in the centre, and beside it a dish filled with large wooden spoons, around both of which the company closed up together in a narrow circle.

A black attendant now appeared mounting the marble stairs, and bearing an enormous bowl of *kouskoussou*, the great staple dish of the country, which he placed in the wooden framework on the floor, that was thus made to serve the purpose of a table. Every guest then provided himself with a spoon, and on a signal from the host the feast began. Simultaneously every spoon was plunged into the well-filled bowl, time after time, and their contents were greedily devoured by the hungry circle of natives. The small fine grain was mixed with sugar and milk, the latter oozing up to the top when the solid part was pressed down by the spoons of the eaters. Round the surface small pieces of boiled mutton were arranged, tender and juicy.

The Europeans were satisfied with a very small quantity, for they felt disgust at eating out of the same vessel with the crowd of Arabs, who pressed inwards for their share, devouring ravenously the coveted mess. Wilton and his friends, notwithstanding that they ceased to eat, considered it courteous to recline patiently in their places until the others had satiated their hunger, although their recumbent postures were far from agreeable. The Marquis de St. Bertrand, however, was not equally considerate, for he remained on the ground but a short time, giving an audible grunt of relief when he found himself again on his feet. This uncalled-for act of unmannerly rudeness greatly outraged Wilton's sense of propriety, and so did the system of espionage that was not ashamed to take advantage of a man's hospitality for the sake of prying into his private affairs. He consequently conceived a strong antipathy against the gay and brilliant Frenchman—a feeling destined to burn with irrepressible intensity hereafter.

An abominable drink, whose basis appeared to be bad honey, was handed round by black domestics as soon as the company rose, followed by one equally atrocious, made principally of sour milk, which latter intensely disgusted Wilton, who chanced to taste it inadvertently.

After a course of orange *sucrée*, heavy unpalatable millet-seed cake, *café noir*, lollypops, and conserves of fruit, the banquet came to an end.

Now the great event of the day drew nigh, and

Selim Mustapha retired to the harem to bring out the little victim—a pretty boy, about twelve years old, dressed in loose white nether garments and a dark-blue brocaded zouave jacket, with a broad red sash tied loosely round his slender waist.

All the female inmates of the harem filed out at the same time upon the flat housetop above, overlooking the galleries where the men were assembled. They were closely shrouded in their white burnouses, with their faces scrupulously concealed; and they kept up a rising swelling chorus of " Lou lou, lou lou," producing a singularly wild and original effect.

The poor child was crying bitterly, and looked desperately frightened; but his father and the Imaum who was to officiate endeavoured to soothe him, as, one on either side, they led him along into the operating chamber. There he was laid down on his back upon a brass bedstead covered with rich Persian rugs, his head between his father's knees, who sat cross-legged behind his back.

As soon as the boy was got ready for the operation, the Imaum produced a pair of pliers and a sharp razor, by means of which he instantaneously made the sufferer one of the Faithful and a true follower of the Prophet. The shrill piercing cry of pain the little fellow uttered was a signal to the ghostlike houris above that the ceremony was concluded, who thereupon broke forth into fresh enthusiastic "lou lous" of delight.

At this moment Wilton chanced to issue forth on the gallery, and looking up to the veiled spectres aloft, he noticed the uncovered face of Kredoudja, whom he instantly recognised as the attendant of Azzahra at the Fountains of the Genii, and previously at the Marengo Gardens. An involuntary exclamation of surprise escaped his lips, and a smile of pleasure lighted up his features as he made the welcome discovery. At the same moment one of the white-draped crowd on high uttered a piercing shriek, and fell back swooning into the arms of those around her.

What would Henry not have given to fly to her aid and clasp her in his arms, for well he knew it was his beloved Azzahra, after whom he had never ceased to pine since that morning at St. Eugène when her beauty first won his heart! Here she was close to him, almost within his grasp; and yet he dared not seek her presence —dared not appear even to notice her as they carried her away, helpless, to her chamber— dared not even ask after her, although now, by this fresh proof, he felt doubly assured of her love. He stood stupefied and speechless, gazing on the spot where she vanished from his sight, until the passing throng from the inner room reminded him that he must move away and take his departure.

Sorrowfully he descended the marble stairs which the feet of his beloved had so often pressed, and he gazed on the beauteous flowers in the spacious courts below, tended perhaps by her, as well as on the fishes and birds doubtless often fed by her fairy hand.

Sad at heart, he passed from this bright abode of luxury into the foul wretched street without, and mingled with the heartless un-sympathizing crowd, who moved along absorbed in the pursuit of gain or pleasure, heedless of the galling agony that was rending his breast asunder.

Still, in spite of the enforced separation from the idol of his love, was it not an immense gain, he thought, to have discovered her abode?—for he could haunt the spot day after day, hour after hour, until she came forth, when he would claim her as his own for ever.

These hopeful reflections gave much comfort to his bleeding heart as he pondered over what had occurred, and he determined to take advantage of the knowledge he had acquired to secure his coveted treasure.

Wrapt up in wild and visionary plans for the future, he descended towards the lower town, threading his way through the panting crowd that toiled up the rugged ascent, and that struggled to force past a crowd of pannier-laden donkeys, which slipped about so as nearly to fall on their heads and knees while driven rapidly downhill along the stony passages under a thick shower of hearty blows from the sticks of their cruel masters.

"You call these streets?" exclaimed a gentleman whose acquaintance he had recently made at table-d'hôte, and who was profusely perspiring. "It is bad enough to drag oneself up such abominable places; but, bless you, I would not have been a Jew in Algiers for a trifle before the French got the country. Then every Turk mounting up these perpendicular alleys could lay hold of the first Hebrew he chanced to meet, and jumping on the back of the browbeaten wretch be borne in luxury to the top."

To Henry, in the excited and impassioned state of his feelings, these uncongenial remarks seemed a cruel and unwarrantable intrusion, so that he found difficulty in returning a polite answer.

"Come and join a picnic to-morrow," continued Edwardes, for such was the name of the gentleman, who by this time had recovered after his toilsome climb. "Antiquarian pursuits are my hobby, and I intend running across the bay in my yacht to explore the ancient city of Rusgunia, on that far point you see opposite. If the ladies of your party care for sailing I shall only be too glad of their company."

The invitation was so cordial and friendly that Henry could not decline accepting, although this arrangement seriously interfered with certain absurd schemes he had in contemplation for watching outside Selim Mustapha's house.

Selfishness formed no part of Wilton's character, and in consequence he was influenced by other and stronger motives than the desire not to offend his new acquaintance by a refusal. He felt it would be unkind towards Olinda and his aunt, still more so towards his beloved sister, to deprive them on his account of an agreeable excursion.

Besides, one day's delay in seeing Azzahra again could be of no vital importance, now that he had so happily discovered where to find her in future. Indeed, it might be more prudent, after all, to keep aloof for a time, lest Selim Mustapha might suspect, after what had occurred on the balcony, that some understanding existed between Azzahra and himself. Were he found so soon afterwards about the house his cause might suffer harm, and he might seriously compromise his beloved Azzahra.

CHAPTER IX.

THE JARDIN D'ESSAI..

AFTER parting from Edwardes, Henry hastened to the Villa Isly, to tell of the projected expedition arranged for the following day should the weather prove favourable.

He found his relatives on the point of stepping into their carriage, and they invited' him to accompany them.

Skirting round the head of one of the adjacent valleys, they soon came out on the well-engineered road that winds up the heights of Mustapha Supérieur, past beautiful villas embowered in gardens of choicest flowers and fruits.

All the way up the ascent, through the vistas between the palms, bananas, caroubiers, almonds, and other rare trees, including the Australian *Eucalyptus globulus*, enchanting glimpses were caught of the snowy crystalline city beneath, laving its feet in the deep blue waves of the sea, and hanging to the sides of the hills like some spotless sparkling glacier.

They pursued this route until they reached the Colonne Voirol on the summit. Here they paused to gaze on the splendid panoramic view, rich with so much beauty and steeped in the gay sunshine, the wild background of the lofty Bou-Zareah heights rising in the distance above. Thence they descended to Birmandraïs, or the Well of the Corsair, a pretty village encircled with shady trees. Continuing along the picturesque road that winds down the richly wooded banks of the Oued Khrenis through the Valley of the Femme Sauvage, they came out at the Ruisseau on the great thoroughfare which runs parallel to the shore, leading eastwards from Algiers to the Kabyle Mountains and, farther on, to the City of Constantine.

Shortly they reached the entrance-gates of the Jardin d'Essai, or Garden of Acclimatisation, maintained by the Government for experimental arboriculture, with the object of rearing trees to plant throughout the colony.

When they had driven some distance round the long carriage-way within the grounds, they alighted, as Miss Thornton wished to find the colony of ostriches from the Desert, hoping to procure some of the birds' feathers for the adornment of her person.

When her aunt and cousin left, Olinda led

Henry up the long avenue of huge palms that intersects the gardens, heedless of the irreverent construction sure to be put on her conduct by Miss Thornton, who was always on the lookout for flirtations.

She gently put her arm within his, and looked up in his face with a soft kind winning smile. She saw the gulf yawning beneath his feet, and she desired to lure him away from the edge of the precipice. Affectionately she told him what deep pain she suffered in beholding his downcast unhappy condition, and how timid she felt in volunteering to interfere, being so much younger than him. Still she could not refrain, she pleaded, from opening her mind and raising her warning voice.

"Alas! I have observed a marked change in you," she continued, "ever since the fatal day you saw that pretty-faced heathen at St. Eugène, and I fear me she has stolen away your heart by her deceptive arts. But surely you could not be so senseless as to think of marrying one about whom you absolutely know nothing—a half-savage, with no education, no refinement, no manner, no religion, no soul?"

"You are utterly mistaken, Olinda," he interposed. "It is absurd to speak thus of a girl whom you yourself praised so much the other day."

"I am not mistaken, Henry," she quickly

responded. "Do not, I implore, be guilty of such folly, such madness! The golden rule of 'like to like' in the selection of life-partners cannot be too closely followed, for a mixed marriage—high mating with low—ever proves a curse to both."

"The day you called my attention to the girl, Olinda," replied Wilton, "you did not speak of her as you do now. Then you were lavish of your praise; now no epithets of contempt are too strong. Whence then this sudden change?"

"Oh, how bitterly I regret my heedless folly!" she sighed, too deeply absorbed in grief to reply. "But for me this Arab would have passed in the crowd unnoticed, and this terrible calamity would not have come."

"Well, Olinda, concealment is vain," resumed Henry. "Once, and that not so long ago, my heart was wholly and solely yours, but you drove me from you. Now I own I do adore that Moslem girl with all my heart and with all my soul. I love her better than my life."

"And you would really make her your wife?"

"That would be out of the question, I suppose," he replied evasively. "My family would most probably disapprove of such an alliance."

"Most undoubtedly they would," she replied with emphasis. "If not to seek her in marriage, then, why encourage this romantic devotion?

Is it right? Is it just to her? Is it just to yourself?"

"I know not," he gasped. "My mind refuses to reason. But live without her I cannot. I must be near her. I must bask in the sunshine of her presence. Apart from her I now feel existence a dreary void. Even just now I beheld her once more for a moment, and, after the proofs of her love I witnessed, I shall never rest contented until she is mine. Why, oh why, did I let her depart that day at the Fountains of the Djins without exchanging even one word?"

Olinda was sad when she heard this fatal declaration, and said: "Too well I knew, alas! that Arab had encompassed you in her trammels. Too well I knew you would refuse to hearken to my friendly counsels. Ah! how rarely is advice received in the spirit with which it is offered!"

"So it happens, Olinda," he sadly answered; "and for this reason, that people are generally the best judges of their own affairs—above all, in matters of love. How is it possible for another to analyze, or even comprehend, the hidden feelings that sway our breasts and constitute our inner life? Your advice is given, I know, from the kindest and best of motives, and I am deeply grateful for your affectionate solicitude; but indeed, Olinda, you would lead me wrong. That girl, I feel persuaded, is not what you suppose. Believe me, she is vastly superior to her race. Believe me, your first impressions were just. Believe me, she is fitted to make any man happy."

"What grounds have you for such a conclusion?" she asked. "What tangible proofs can you show? You know you have none beyond mere surmise," she added after a pause, seeing he could offer no reply. "Well you know how these Mahometan women are reared in ignorance and inanity, surrounded though they may be by wealth and splendour, without one particle of refinement or exalted feeling, without one particle of intellectual culture. You know their sole education is the knowledge of adorning their persons and intriguing, their sole morality a lock and key. Oh! Henry, take not such an one to wife, for to wed her you too surely intend, notwithstanding your denial; aught else you are too honourable to contemplate. Lean not on such a broken reed. Wreck not your happiness, disgrace not your family, by such incomprehensible infatuation. Had this happened to a mere boy, like my young brother, for example, I could forgive his committing love at first sight; but you have arrived at man's estate, and you are expected to think of something more than a pretty face in the selection of a life-companion."

Then Henry gently interrupted, and told of the scene that occurred in the house of Azzahra's father, and of the Oriental pride and splendour with which the girl whom she despised as so humble was surrounded. He told her that after the evidence he had received, slight though it might be, he knew he was beloved. "And when woman loves," he added, passing by unnoticed her unwelcome observations, "a man can mould her to his will."

The Marquis de St. Bertrand here met them, lounging round the grounds with a brother officer in his regiment, and, as he passed, saluted Olinda with formal politeness; but directly he turned and scowled back with a glance of defiant hatred at her and her cousin, engaged, as he believed, in the happy mysteries of courtship. How amazed he would have felt could he have looked within and seen the severing heartburnings to which they were both a prey!

"Always after something nice, St. Bertrand," exclaimed his friend in a bantering strain. "*Parole d'honneur*, I know none with so keen an eye and such a weasel scent for lighting upon *piquante* beauty. You are a true *bon enfant, mon ami*—'one jolly dog,' as the Meess would say."

"Why, I never met the young lady before, except on one occasion," answered Raoul, anxious to conceal his anger at being supplanted.

"Bah! You mean, though, to meet her often again. Just now you would have joined her, but you saw she was flirting with that fellow, and you got jealous. I know your ways, *mon camarade.* I know you would not have given that black look and ground your teeth did you not think he was crossing your path."

"Well, I own you are right, Auguste," said his friend, laughing. "I am desperately in love with this fair blonde, and, what is more, I mean to gain her. She is a glorious magnificent girl!"

"That she is," replied Auguste, "and will make a rare fine wife." And he added: "You intend to marry her, of course?"

"*Cela depend, mon ami,*" the other answered. "Marriage means milliners' bills, and rent and taxes, and liveried servants, and carriages and horses, and butchers and bakers, and all the rest. If she has a large fortune, well and good; but you know, Auguste, that my finances are by no means adequate for the position I ought to occupy as a Benedict, though ample for a *garçon's* life in a barrack-room."

"That means that should she prove penniless you will turn her adrift to pine and die of a broken heart?"

"Not a bit of it," interrupted St. Bertrand. "Sooner than be guilty of such base cruel barbarity, if I cannot marry, I will do the next best thing."

"You overlook the prudence and reserve of these young English ladies," Auguste went on. "The proposal would be received as an insult, 'and you would be shot by some father or brother for your impertinence."

"The Anglaises are not what they used to be," rejoined Raoul. "They allow freedoms that were formerly looked upon as affronts, and at *double entendre* they are quite at home. As to a duel, there is no such thing in England now; the cowards will not fight."

"You estimate not our foreign friends aright," answered Auguste. "Neither women nor men are what you suppose."

"They are, though, Pécoul," exclaimed his comrade; "I know them well."

"*Eh bien!* You are a good authority in these matters," Pécoul replied, shrugging his shoulders; "but, nevertheless, I say you will fail."

"Very probably I may fail by fair means; but, sooner than own myself vanquished and be defrauded of the prize I covet, I will resort to other and surer measures."

"Bravely spoken!" Auguste continued. "When the hour arrives, should you require aid, reckon upon me."

"Thanks, a thousand times!" exclaimed St. Bertrand, warmly grasping the hand of his comrade; "I ever knew you were a kind and sincere friend."

Little suspecting the hellish machinations that occupied the thoughts of the gay hussar, Olinda regretted that he had not stopped, to continue an acquaintanceship she had found so agreeable.

Renewing the conversation with Wilton, she went on to comment on what he had just said.

"But wherefore marry one you would have to mould to your will?" she quickly asked. "Why become a schoolmaster to your wife? Why waste your time endeavouring to tame a savage, and to indoctrinate her, in defiance of all her early habits and preconceived notions, with European ideas and manners? Remember, Henry, the good old adage about the silken purse and the sow's ear."

"But have I said I would marry her?" he interrupted. "And, as regards your denunciations, I cannot get you to comprehend that Azzahra has been cradled in luxury and reared in affluence such as neither you nor I have ever experienced."

"Mould a woman to your will, forsooth!" she exclaimed, taking no note of his interruption. "You know not what a wild hazardous experiment you would try. Far from exhibiting gratitude, this untamed creature will hate you for detecting and correcting her deficiencies. Your well-meant efforts to refine her mind and to educate her up to the level of your ideal standard will be deemed an insult and an outrage. Her pride will be mortified because she does not seem perfect in your sight. She will angrily conclude that you despise her inferiority, that you consider her too far beneath you to deserve your love. Woman adores being praised and flattered. To her admiration is life, how pure and virtuous soever she may be. It is the air she breathes, the food she exists on. It is her one great aim and object in life. I deny not that I love praise myself. Every woman with high spirit loves it—praise not from strangers, which would be impertinence, but praise from those we love. Fail to gratify this desire, abstain from all approving commendation, point out besides foibles and shortcomings, and what must be the inevitable result? Confidence will be destroyed, and an impassable barrier will be reared up that will make the lives of both simply unbearable. Indeed, your arguments go to prove, as clearly as aught I can say, the uncertainty you yourself feel as to the wisdom of your determination. One moment you say this poor heathen is calculated to make you happy, and the next, almost in the same breath, you allow that you will have to lift her up in the social scale ere she is fit to be even a companion. Can you not see the folly of such glaring contradictions and inconsistencies? Can you not see the slough before your eyes into which you are bent on plunging yourself and your fortunes? Do think dispassionately, Henry, of what I say, and weigh well the consequences of the step you contemplate, before you commit yourself irretrievably to ruin and despair."

"I am prepared to run all hazards, all risks, for her sake," he said with energy. "I love her devotedly, Olinda; I love her madly!"

"Yes, you believe you love her," said Olinda in reply, sadly shaking her head. "The other day you believed you loved me madly, but you were mistaken. Why should you not be mistaken again? What guarantee have you that this is not another transient evanescent fancy, such as most experience often through life? The fancy soon passes away, to leave no scar behind, to give no pain to the heart; and the once-beloved object, for whom life would have been gladly sacrificed, is forgotten as though never clothed with any real existence. How can you say this will not happen in your case? How can you say that prudence will not assert her sway, after the heyday of passion has passed, to accuse you of gross heedless folly in suffering yourself to be carried away thus helplessly to destruction? Did I not love you as my cousin, Henry, and love you very much, I would not speak thus frankly. But I cannot, without remonstrance, see your noble nature linked to one so far—so very far—beneath you, and whom you yourself acknowledge you ought not to wed."

"You tell me I thought I loved you once, Olinda, but was mistaken," he answered. "I was not mistaken. I loved you dearly, Olinda. I esteemed you; I honoured you; I adored you. I thought you all that man could desire in woman. I wondered at your talents, your accomplishments, your virtues, as though you were some bright being descended to earth from a happier sphere. But I found you loved me not in return. You sympathized not with me, you did not conceal that you deemed me unfit to mate with, and you coldly repulsed my declarations of attachment. What man could tamely submit to hear woman speak like this, to hear her class him as belonging to a lower grade, to hear her spurn him as unworthy of obtaining her hand? No, Olinda. Wrongs such as these deaden and freeze the heart, and mine has become dead and frozen. But I blame you not. You rate yourself far above me, and look for a husband more worthy of your choice. You are justified in holding these opinions, and I am likewise justified in withdrawing my affections from where they were so egregiously misplaced. Man is not worthy of the name that hangs about a woman and fawns upon her after she has plainly intimated that he is no longer acceptable. Had you, however, considered me worthy of your love, I should have been your devoted slave until death. But it was not to be. Accuse me

not, then, of fickleness, Olinda. It is neither
right nor just. You must know that such is not
my nature."

"I accused you not of fickleness," she gently
pleaded. "I said you fancied you were in love
when you were not. I told you, not that you
would change, but that you would discover your
error of judgment, and my estimate is now
proved correct. Oh! sincerely do I pray that
you may not have cause to repent of your headstrong blindness, should you take this Arab to
wife. Were I to see you unhappy I should ever
reproach myself for repulsing you, and thereby
forcing you into this unequal alliance."

"But had you condescended to marry me, the
alliance would have been still more unequal,"
he replied rather bitterly; for he was irritated
afresh against his cousin for her disparaging
manner of alluding to Azzahra, and therefore
made no allowance for the fond spirit in which
she spoke.

"Oh! taunt me not thus, Henry," she urged,
turning away her face to hide a tell-tale tear.
"Could you know how you wound my feelings
you would abstain from such cruel remarks."

"I but repeat what you have many times told
me yourself," he replied, "and I acknowledge
the justice of your decision."

Olinda saw he was bent on rushing to his
doom, but she made one more effort. Once

again she appealed to him, by his former love, to tear himself away from this woman, with whom he had not one idea in common. But he heeded her not.

"Waste not more words, I beseech you," he exclaimed with decision. "My resolve is taken —so firmly taken that no entreaties can turn me from my purpose of following this fair creature and winning her, if I can. I pine after the innocent looking, unspoilt child of nature, unversed in the ways of the world, reared under the protecting shadow of her father's roof. How sweet to claim such a pure fair being as one's own, whose ear had never before hearkened to the voice of love, who had never been wooed by another!"

His headlong passion held such mastery that his cousin's warning denunciations, far from checking the flame, made it burn all the brighter. He commenced even to regard Olinda's interference with suspicion—to surmise that she had become jealous, that she was acting a part, that she was endeavouring to keep him still dangling in her train as a servile though discarded admirer.

What blindness, to harbour these calumnious unworthy thoughts of his proud honourable cousin! He forgot her noble nature. He forgot how incapable she was of practising such arts, of betraying such narrow-minded deception.

What blindness, not to perceive that deep,

warm-hearted, unselfish affection alone prompted her to interest herself on his behalf!

Her keen woman's instinct detected that she was misunderstood, that she was suspected of selfish motives—a discovery which deeply wounded her; for she abhorred the very mention of flirtation, and looked with scorn at women who gave encouragement, merely to get admiration, to lovers whose pretensions they were determined never to entertain. Such poor triumphs her virtuous mind regarded, and rightly, in the light of wanton heartless outrages against society, meriting universal execration.

It was with a sensation of relief, then, that she perceived Alice Thornton and Geraldine coming towards them up the long walk of gigantic bamboos which intersects at right-angles the palm-avenue where she and Wilton were walking. She felt glad that this painful colloquy had come to a close, for she saw she could not stem the tide. She could but hope that time would effect what she had failed to accomplish.

"Not a word to them," he whispered, as Olinda went forward to meet her aunt.

"Rely on me," she answered; "I will keep your secret safe."

As they went on, Miss Thornton, with her wonted heedless levity, rallied her nephew and niece on the lovemaking she concluded had been carried on during her absence, which was singularly infelicitous under the circumstances, but which greatly took the fancy of Geraldine, who delighted in observing and discussing flirtations. But Wilton paid back his aunt's raillery with similar good-humoured badinage.

"My dear Aunt Alice," he cried out with a hearty laugh, "you judge everybody by yourself. Because you get up flirtations whenever you are offered a chance, it by no means follows that we quiet steady young people must follow your example. We are far too prudent, rest assured, to attempt anything so ridiculous."

But the old lady's inconsiderate frolic brought scalding tears to the eyes of Olinda, which she vainly essayed to repress. From her aunt and Geraldine she succeeded in concealing her weakness, but not from Henry, whose heart softened again towards his fair cousin, as he noticed her silent bitter grief. When he looked upon her sweet, angelic, saddened face he freely pardoned her hostility against Azzahra, which just before had so exasperated his mind. He longed to put his arm round her, as of old, and ask forgiveness for the unkind intemperate words he had used— for his obtuseness in failing to recognise that her disparaging warnings, mortifying though he felt them, were offered solely through warm and disinterested affection. This tender solicitude of hers now appeared in its true colours before his eyes, and he felt thankful that so deep an interest should be taken by another in his welfare. Though he had failed to secure Olinda's love, yet it flattered him, it soothed him, to know that, as a relation at least, she regarded him with profound attachment.

His heart overflowing with these thoughts, he resolved that when next they chanced to be alone together he would make submission and sue for pardon.

How woman's strength lies in her weakness! In tears she is omnipotent.

Olinda too, on her part, began to examine her feelings and to ask herself searching questions. Womanlike, now that she believed Wilton lost to her for ever, she relented, and felt grieved at her hardness of heart.

Had she acted aright, she wondered, in chilling this brave manly nature? Had she been wise in rejecting his suit—in repelling one whose chivalrous integrity was above all suspicion? Though hereafter she might meet a lover more talented, more brilliant, more accomplished, was she sure to find the same nobleness of character, the same depth of genuine feeling, the same exalted standard of virtue and honour?

Thus they continued to walk on, side by side, through the wondrous wealth of tropical trees and plants, softened and drawn nearer together again, although a fathomless abyss, impassable to both, yawned between them still.

The wild whirlwinds of emotion sweeping through the breasts of her companions were little suspected by the shallow unobservant mind of Alice Thornton, but the eyes of Geraldine were less dull of perception. That precocious young lady was a considerable adept at flirtation, and *au courant* far beyond her years in affairs of the heart.

The altered manner as well as the saddened looks of her brother and cousin were speedily detected by her quick glance, but she failed to discover the intensity or even the nature of their mental anguish. She concluded that one of those pretty lovers' quarrels she read about had occurred, which were so delightful to heal up, and which always made the happy belligerents so lavish of love as soon as the fitful breeze had ceased to ruffle the surface of the waters. Until now her mind misgave her as to whether any actual engagement existed between the two. No longer could she doubt. So she settled definitively in her mind that Olinda was destined to be her sister as well as her cousin.

"How could it be otherwise?" she reasoned. "They surely must be very far gone indeed to get up such a serious quarrel."

Thus, all misunderstanding one another and absorbed in their own respective contemplations, the party re-entered their carriage.

Passing the dense plantations of large

bananas—many. of whose lofty tender stems,
laden with widely branching fern-like leaves,
were supported by tall square wooden frames,
and whose pendant fruits were encased in small
woollen bags to prevent their falling to the
ground, as well as to keep off the chill of any
frost-laden blast at early morn—they found themselves on the shore of the Mediterranean, opposite a grove of gigantic aloes, close to which
stood a small *café maure* beneath the huge leaves
of some date-palms.

On a bench beneath these large trees a
malevolent looking swarthy Arab with a young
veiled girl and her black attendant were sipping
coffee.

When Olinda perceived them she recognised Kredoudja she turned deadly pale in a
moment, so as to attract the notice of Wilton,
who looked to learn the cause of this sudden
change. Then he beheld his beloved Azzahra
fondly gazing on him as she sat by her father's
side.

Oh! what agony for each to be thus close to
the beloved object without daring even to make
a sign of recognition!—both burning to rush to
each other, yet cruelly compelled to remain
aloof!

Henry continued to keep his eyes fixed on the
white burnouses of Azzahra and Selim Mustapha
until the grove of aloes hid them from his sight.

"I see you!" exclaimed Geraldine to Henry with a merry twinkle of her eye. "That's the girl that fell in love with you the other day when the band was playing. What a pity her father is with her to-day! Only for that, you might get out and have a nice flirtation under those palms, with nobody to watch you. You would not mind, Olinda, would you?"

A look from Olinda made the young lady stop short in mid-career; but why she should be debarred from making fun of her brother, for her special amusement, she could not comprehend.

How oft are daggers thus plunged into the bleeding heart by a heedless word or jest! What bitter agony the little maid caused to the fallen Guinevere on the terrace at Amesbury by her silly babbling tongue!

As they turned off the highroad to mount the steep ascent to Isly, close to the Constantine Gate, they found the way choked by a crowd of Kabyles and camels, which compelled them to halt. While thus detained Geraldine seized the opportunity so propitiously offered to horrify her aunt.

"What fun, Aunt Alice, to have been here in the time of the Turks," she exclaimed, laughing, "when culprits were impaled or suspended on hooks to die on the walls of that city-gate yonder! Imagine a row of human heads grinning at you from those battlements, horrid and gory!"

"For goodness' sake, child," exclaimed Miss Thornton, shuddering, "do not mention such hideous barbarities; you make my blood run cold!"

While they were thus blocked in the crowd, Edwardes came alongside the carriage, and begged of Wilton to present him to the ladies, as they were to be his guests so soon on board the yacht—a request cheerfully accorded by Henry, for he appreciated more and more every time they met the sterling merits of his new acquaintance.

Edwardes's conversation was so agreeable and his manners were so attractive that, although no longer young, he was highly appreciated by the ladies, especially Miss Thornton, who declared enthusiastically, after he left, that he was one of the most charming delicious men she had ever laid eyes on.

This outburst of admiration vastly entertained Geraldine, who had often enjoyed similar romantic sallies on the part of her maiden aunt, and who laughed heartily at the transparent coquetry of the worthy old lady.

As for Olinda and Wilton, they were too deeply absorbed in their own reflections to enjoy their aunt's absurdities, or the glaring way in which she ogled the good-looking stranger. Sadly the two bade adieu for the day, for both felt misgivings as to the past, the present, and the future. Both doubted the prudence of their decision, though they owned that now the past could never be recalled. Both likewise looked forward to the future with a slight quivering of apprehension. Of the two Wilton was the more sanguine. Of Azzahra's love he entertained not a doubt. Yet, though so confident, there were moments came when reason reasserted its sway, and when he could not deny that his mind would be more at ease after confirmation from her own lips of his belief that she was worthy to become his wife, did he finally resolve on marriage. This question of marriage was a problem he knew pressed for solution, yet it was one he felt unable to solve, and wished to avoid solving.

What if, notwithstanding Azzahra's proud high-bred mien and the luxurious opulence of her position in life, she should prove unfitted for companionship with Olinda, perchance unfitted to be even presented! What if she were shunned, despised, mocked, hunted down—by his own flesh-and-blood too!—by a woman who had slighted himself and refused to bestow on him her hand!

The thought was too horrible. It maddened him. It well nigh drove him to despair.

CHAPTER X.

THE CONSPIRATORS.

No sooner had the stranger guests departed from Selim Mustapha's abode, than he collected around him his fellow-conspirators in a secluded part of the marble court below, where a cool grotto beside a crystal brook shaded by the lofty perfumed orange-trees offered a retreat secure from interruption.

Here he whispered, as they seated themselves on rich orient carpets, the important intelligence that he would shortly depart on his return to the Desert, whither they should follow, but at intervals of a few days, so as not to excite suspicion.

He gave them instructions how they were to cross the Tell by different routes—some by Tlemcen; some by Milianah and Teniet-el-Hâad, by which line he himself would follow; some by Medeah, some by Laghouat, and some by Constantine and Biskara; and how, as they passed, they were in secret to give the signal for revolt and to gain adherents by the way. All were to rendezvous in one moon at the Plains of Sersou, whence their armed band would sweep through the Sahara from Morocco to Tunis, spreading destruction and consternation from frontier to frontier.

"The hour has struck," he proudly continued, raising aloft his right hand and smiting upon his breast, "when the haughty oppressor shall be driven from the land! He thinks we are cowed; he thinks we are down-trodden; he thinks we are base, abject, craven slaves, subservient to his lordly will. But he knows not the proud spirit of our tribes. He knows not the wild passion for vengeance that burns in the breasts of the Children of the Free. He knows not of the mighty power wielded by this right arm, nor of the thousands of patriot warriors I can summon to my standard. I go, my friends, to array a glorious armament, that shall trample the Giaour to perdition!"

"Reflect, O Selim Mustapha," interrupted the discreet Al-Mansour, "upon the might in battle of the power you are going to defy. How can our wild untrained nomads and mountaineers stand up in fight against sixty thousand disciplined European warriors? It means destruction, Selim Mustapha—it means death!"

"But we will not stand up against them—not,

at least, in the open field," replied his chief. " We will retreat before them. We will draw them after us into the depths of the desert, where want and starvation await them, and where we can slay them at our will."

"Yes—slay a thousand or fifteen hundred in cold blood, the greatest number that need or that could pursue so far away from their re- sources," Al-Mansour retorted with a bitter scornful laugh. " And will that advance your cause ? Most certainly not. For every Frank you put to the sword a dozen natives will perish, to strike terror into our conquered race. Rush not into this mad enterprise. Draw not down on our unhappy persecuted creed the deadly, the resistless vengeance of our foes. Take warn- ing, O Selim Mustapha, son of Ben-Eutemi ! None more gladly than I would trample down the hated tyrants, as you all can testify— none more gladly make them to bite the dust. But well know I that, for the present, the attempt would be insensate folly. The day may come when the foul infidel will writhe in agony, humbled and crushed to the earth by some other accursed nation of Europe. Then will come our opportunity. Then will we rise in our might, and win back our dear native land from the grasp of the perjured invader."

A slight murmur of approval ran round as he finished, to the dismay of Selim Mustapha, who thus beheld his vision of victory and glory threatened with unexpected extinction. Furious with hatred and rage, he resolved to stamp out mercilessly these mutinous symptoms, even to the sacrifice of his old and valued friend.

"Await then your opportunity, Al-Mansour, which will never come," he answered, a storm of contemptuous fury sweeping across his impassioned features. "Wait, and bask here in safety with the women and children, beneath the approving smiles of your masters, whilst we go forth to fight your battles—to cover ourselves with glory and renown !"

"Your taunts move me not," Al-Mansour calmly observed. "I will not go out with you to battle in a hopeless cause, which can only result in the useless shedding of blood. Show me a way to conquer, show me even any reasonable grounds for hope, and I will fight beside you to the death. But you know your mission is hopeless. You. know your enemy can crush you whenever you venture within his grasp. You know your only chance of safety is to fly before his face. Can you succeed where the mighty Emir himself failed, although he waged war under conditions immeasurably more advantageous ? Where are your arms ? Where are your field-guns ? Where are your trained disciplined battalions ? Where is the

Smala for storing your arms and for the manufacture of your military *matériel ?* "

" Abd-el-Kader failed because he committed
the fatal blunder of taking up his positions in
the Tell," pursued Selim Mustapha, evading a
direct reply to these searching unwelcome
questions. " Had he made the Desert his base of
operations, with his headquarters away among
the unapproachable Oases of the South, dis-
patching flying columns of cavalry to surprise
unguarded posts, to waylay convoys, to sack,
burn, and destroy—had he, in short, established
his Smala in the country of the M'Zabites,
instead of in the Tell, he would have rendered
colonisation impossible. He would have forced
the French to abandon a country where they were
driven to desperation by a foe they could never
approach. Thus would he have triumphed, in
place of falling a prisoner into the hands of
his enemies, to pass a sad existence of exile far
away from the land of his fathers."

" And did not the Emir carry on this guerilla
warfare ?" Al-Mansour retorted. " Did he not
long continue to harass the French from his
mountain fastness on the Wan-nash-Reese, and
to set them at defiance ? Relying on the support of this stronghold in the Ouanseris Mountains, did he not besiege the neighbouring city
of Milianah ? Was not the garrison of that
fortress reduced by famine, disease, and slaughter

throughout the winter from twelve hundred to five hundred, of whom four hundred were invalided in hospital? And the survivors, were they not on the point of surrendering, when the siege was raised by Changarnier at the head of a powerful relieving army? But of what value or account were these brilliant exploits? What did these bold tactics avail when the enemy followed in pursuit? Did his almost impregnable position—his eyry on the Wan-nash-Reese—serve to keep off the enemy? You know it did not. You know the Christians mounted by the Valley of the Silver River, capturing the whole of our forces, along with their flocks and herds—the Emir himself only escaping through the fleetness of his black Arab mare."

"I know that but for treachery the Franks would have failed," Selim Mustapha exultingly answered. "Had not that accursed dog of a Kabyle pointed out the way to surround the mountain, and so to starve the Emir into surrender, our camp could never have been taken. We succumbed to cowardly stratagem, not to bravery or skill in fair open fight. Had it not been for this base treason, we should have continued to hurl down rocks on the heads of the attacking army, as they strove to clamber up the inaccessible heights of the Oued Fodda, annihilating reinforcement after reinforcement."

Selim Mustapha heard a sound close at hand,

and cautiously crept out to discover the cause. But the noise merely proceeded from his favourite greyhound, Karakouch, walking across the pavement of the court, and he returned to resume the important conference.

" On the heights of Mouzaïa, again," resumed Al-Mansour, "what a gallant stand our army made, and what havoc they caused in the enemy's ranks before he gained the victory ! "

"But he did gain the victory," Selim Mustapha proudly replied. "And why did he gain the victory? Because we made a stand and awaited his attack. Had we fallen back on the trackless wastes of sand he never would have conquered. That is the policy I mean to follow —a policy that has never yet been tried—and I know it will triumph. Who will join my standard, and march to drive the Christians from our shores ? "

A wild outburst of applause from the group of his friends greeted this martial appeal to arms, all of whom solemnly pledged themselves to meet him in the Desert at the appointed time, never to quit the saddle until victory was theirs.

Al-Mansour even gave in his adhesion, when he found his prudent counsels could not stay the wild project ; for he dearly loved his native country, and shrank from bearing the reputation of a traitor—a construction he foresaw would be put upon his conduct were he to persist in opposition to what were clearly the wishes of all present, carried away by the enthusiasm of their leader.

Although his comrades felt he was thus joining their ranks reluctantly, and as it were under protest, his adhesion was accounted a valuable gain; for they knew well that, once embarked in an enterprise, he was not the man to look back with a wavering or despondent heart.

Then Selim Mustapha lifted up his hand, invoking the blessing of Allah upon their undertaking, and praying that bitterest curses might attend on traitors to the glorious cause of liberty—prayers in which every one present joined with a low murmur of assent.

"It rejoices me, O Al-Mansour, that you will be found in our ranks," Selim Mustapha resumed. "My favourite child Azzahra will accompany me, and I should blush to see you shrink from deeds of valour that a woman longs to take part in. She has a brave heart, Al-Mansour, and will bear herself nobly in the hour of trial. The girl I take with me because I will not leave her—the idol of my heart, the pride of my life—at the mercy of the Christian dogs in Algiers, should they discover that I am Si Sala, the terrible conquering chieftain of the Desert, of whom they stand in such dread. I choose not that she should perchance be seized and kept a hostage, to force me into submission and surrender. Were the rest taken the blow would be crushing, but the loss of Azzahra would drive me to despair."

"The Franks would not act thus," interposed Al-Mansour. "Still, for other reasons, it will be well to remove your daughter far away."

"For other reasons? What other reasons?" savagely demanded Selim Mustapha.

"Even now I saw her exchange signals with one of your Christian guests," Al-Mansour frigidly answered.

He was enraged in his heart at the mortifying covert sneers of Selim Mustapha in contrasting his conduct with that of a woman, and he adopted this base method of gratifying his thirst for revenge. And the cowardly shaft took deadly effect, for it struck in a vital spot.

"How know you it was Azzahra?" Selim Mustapha shrieked out, livid with furious rage. "How distinguish, when all were veiled? Speak, Al-Mansour; and, at your peril, tell the truth."

"The young Negress was beside her," the other calmly replied, "whom you yourself have pointed out as her constant attendant."

"What saw you, then? What passed between my child and this dog of a Christian?" breathlessly gasped the unhappy father, stricken down and crushed by what he heard.

"When I came out on the balcony with the Christian, after we had witnessed the sacred ceremony," Al-Mansour answered coldly, "he suddenly started, uttered a slight exclamation, and held up his hands on looking at your women above; whereupon one of the youngest—Azzahra, as I believe—gave a faint cry and fell senseless on the floor. No more I saw, for she was quickly lifted up and carried away into the harem."

"Woe is me, wretched man that I am!" Selim exclaimed in deep anguish. "Sooner let her perish in the sea or in the flames, sooner let her be torn into ten thousand fragments, than become a prey to the Giaour! Oh, Al-Mansour, you could not have seen aright? My Azzahra! —the fairest pearl of my heart, the sweetest rose of my garden!—would not bring disgrace on her father's house by such shameless wantonness. She would not turn aside from her race, and give herself up to the foul embraces of the Infidel. I cannot believe in guilt, in base ingratitude like this—the child on whom I have lavished such boundless love!"

"Alas, my brother, such is life!" answered the sage Al-Mansour. "The beloved object on whom we bestow our best affections, and on whose devotion we rely with unswerving faith, deserts us with cruel heartlessness—nay more, surveys our agony and despair with cold remorseless composure. Fix not then your heart on earthly bliss, O friend of my youth, or disappointment will be your portion. Do you doubt the truth of what I say? Go, ask your daughter; she is of age to speak for herself."

Sad at heart, Selim Mustapha hastened above to the harem, to seek his child.

A crowd still gathered around her, but he could clearly gather from their remarks that they guessed not what Al-Mansour declared to be the cause of her sudden indisposition. Greatly was his mind relieved at this discovery, for well he knew the jealousy with which his wives regarded the child of his former favourite, and how gladly they would seize an opportunity of hunting her down to perdition.

To propitiate them he had banished for ever the wife so tenderly beloved; but they were not contented by even that great sacrifice, continuing to visit their hatred of the mother upon her unoffending child.

So he would not that they knew his daughter was suspected of giving her love to a Christian. They had accused the mother of this crime, but they must not get an opportunity of laying such a foul charge at the door of her offspring.

Still he feared to meet Azzahra—feared the terrible accusation might prove true—feared she might, in her artlessness, confess the dreaded secret that she loved this man.

The hesitation, and aversion even, she had

displayed when he spoke of bestowing her in marriage recurred to his recollection, and made him tremble. Could this be the reason, he wondered, why she expressed such reluctance to wed with one of her own race?

Azzahra at length recovered consciousness. Putting his arm gently round her, he led her slowly into his own apartments. Then he questioned her tenderly about the scene described by Al-Mansour, connecting her swoon with the gestures of his foreign guest.

With downcast look and trembling voice she replied, for she recoiled from the deception that was inevitable. While owning the correctness of Al-Mansour's statement as to what occurred, she repudiated the inferences he drew. She earnestly assured her father with the most solemn asseverations that nervousness alone had overcome her, startled at the suddenness of Wilton's gesticulation, which had filled her with alarm. She passionately declared that she knew not the man, that he was a perfect stranger, that she had never spoken to him even one word, and that no signal of any description whatever had passed.

The earnest artless manner in which Azzahra gave her father these assurances, and the shame she appeared to feel at having been suspected, carried conviction to the mind of the doting parent; and, imprinting a kiss on her warm glowing cheek, he professed full reliance on her truthfulness and purity.

Ah! he knew not what was passing within that little fluttering bosom. He knew not what ardent love for the Christian possessed her heart now she had proof that the handsome foreigner returned her affection; for was it not evident that he had traced her steps to her home, and had taken advantage of the opportunity this ceremony offered for seeing and meeting her again? That such was his object in coming she doubted not for a moment; and was it not the strongest proof he could give of his love?

But all this lay hidden from the eyes of Selim Mustapha. He suspected not how she honoured the European because he was an European, nor what contempt she felt for the ignorant brutish voluptuaries of her own people. He suspected not how the favoured child of his bosom was betraying him under the cloak of guileless simplicity. He suspected not that she knew the secret that speech was given to us to conceal our thoughts.

Returning to his friends reassured by Azzahra's protestations, and relieved from the weight of shame imported by the words of Al-Mansour, he repeated with a father's honest pride the explanation his child had given.

But the prudent Al-Mansour well knew the

female heart, and trusted **not**. He suspected still, but he held his peace.

After explaining all final arrangements for the ensuing campaign, and giving instructions for their guidance, he dismissed his colleagues in rebellion, impressing on them the necessity for strict caution, and urging them to meet punctually at the appointed rendezvous in the heart of the Desert.

CHAPTER XI.

ILL-TIMED AFFECTION.

WHEN Selim Mustapha left his daughter she clapped her hands for Kredoudja, who swiftly responded to the summons.

Exhausted by the trying scenes she had passed through, and shedding scalding tears of regret at her approaching departure from the spot that contained him she now so deeply loved, Azzahra reclined upon cushions spread on a crimson velvet ottoman which occupied a recess in the chamber; for she was still too languid and weak to sit upright, as was her wont, on the gaily coloured carpets that lay extended along the floor.

Her mind was worn-out by excitement, and she sighed for a comforter in her distress. She knew how vain it was to conceal from Kredoudja the passion she felt for Wilton now, for she had already told the Black at the Ayoun-Beni-Menad with what admiration the handsome European even then had filled her breast. She knew that

when he looked up from the balcony the Negress
had recognised him as the same before whom
her mistress had unveiled. She knew the girl
perceived that her agitation and the consequent
catastrophe were caused by his sudden appearance beneath her feet. So she feared not to
lay bare her mind and confide to the faithful
Soudanese the mental anguish she endured at
the thought of departing without an opportunity
to hold sweet communion with the object of her
devotion. Perhaps, she sighed, he might depart
to Europe before her return from the Desert, and
then she would never see his face again.

Bitterly now she bewailed her fate in having
irrevocably pledged herself to accompany her
father in his wanderings, in having induced him
to make the fatal proposal by the enthusiastic
praise he had overheard of wild Arab life.

Now it was too late to draw back, for what
excuse could she frame to account for such a
speedy change in her thoughts and plans that
would not fill the mind of her parent with suspicions and misgivings—especially since he
had so incomprehensibly discovered what caused
her to swoon upon the housetop ? She had succeeded in disarming his suspicions and removing
his doubts, it was true ; but how easily might the
smouldering embers be fanned and kindled into
a flame again ; how readily might he connect
her altered intentions with the scene that had

occurred, and with the reports that he had heard?

Long she pondered over the course she should pursue. How was she to act in this grievous strait? How secure her lover without transgressing her filial duty and forfeiting her father's favour?

Ah! poor feeble human nature! The longer she reflected, and the more she doubted, the weaker became the claims of filial duty and desire for parental favour; the more powerful became the influence drawing her towards her loved Giaour, and the deeper his image became engraven on her heart. Were she only certain of his constancy, she thought, she could even dare to remain and brave her father's wrath.

But, alas! he might fail to seek her out again. Then what would be her fate after flinging from her the love of her father and drawing down his anger in vain?

In her distress she helplessly appealed to Kredoudja for comfort and advice.

"Oh, Kredoudja!" she plaintively sobbed, "did I feel assured of this Christian's love I would risk all for his sake. But how am I to tell? In my soul I believe him true, yet have I read that men are faithless and deceive."

"Would that to-morrow had been the morning for consulting the Djins!" sorrowfully ejaculated the Negress. "We could have repaired

again to the Ayoun-Beni-Menad at St. Eugène
to learn your destiny before our journey commenced. Now, alas! this resource is denied us.
Ere Wednesday comes round again we shall be
far away."

"Too true—too true!" Azzahra answered
sadly. "Oh! what would I not give to ask counsel once more of the evil spirits! Kredoudja, I
am overwhelmed with uncertainty and sorrow.
Before me I behold only blank despair!"

And the unhappy girl began to weep afresh,
burying her face in her hands and sobbing aloud.

"To-night a great Derdeba of our tribes will
take place at the house of my uncle in the Rue
Kattarandjil," whispered Kredoudja, sorrowful
at beholding the tribulation of her mistress,
"where several of 'the possessed' will be present, who can divine with certainty the events of
the future. How I wish you could accompany
me there! But it would be madness to venture
forth at night. Were you missed by your
father, after the events of the day, he could not
be persuaded that you had not gone to meet the
Christian."

"I care not what risks I run," exclaimed
Azzahra with decision, springing up from the
couch where she reclined; "I will go with you.
My brain is throbbing with excitement and
despair. The torture of suspense is greater than
I am able to endure. Come what may, Kre-

doudja, you shall take me along with you to-night. Often have I heard of the wonders of your Derdebas, and long have I desired to attend those marvellous scenes."

"You ever declared yourself a disbeliever in magic," pleaded the Black, "or I should have invited you to join me in witnessing the gatherings of my people, and their triumphs in the arts of sorcery, at a time when our absence together could not have given rise to remark."

"I acknowledge," Azzahra replied, "that in my studies I was taught to regard such familiar intercourse with the powers of darkness as pernicious and criminal; but, Kredoudja, my heart has begun to hanker after the supernatural. What I witnessed at the Ayoun-Beni-Menad exerted profound influence. It has so scattered to the winds the crude theories I had learned that the thirst for diving into the mysteries of the future gains strength within me from day to day."

"Great is my joy, my darling beloved mistress," exclaimed the Negress, shedding tears of delight, "to find that you are casting off from you the works of darkness and the false belief of the detested Christians. Oh! leave not the faith of your forefathers—the only true religion on earth! Spurn, as you would poison, the blasphemous accursed creed of the infidels, who believe not in the holy name of the Prophet!"

"But why do you extol Mahometanism?" Azzahra called out, interrupting her. "Your sacred rites were never inculcated by Mahomet; they are not even named in the Koran."

"True," replied the Soudanese; "but these holy mysteries are the relics of our ancient worship — a worship older far than either Mahometanism or Christianity. Were they not part of a pure and holy faith, could they have survived, think you, the persecutions and cruelties our ancestors were subjected to by their Turkish masters, when they were dragged as slaves from their happy homes in the far South, and forced to embrace Islamism under the threat of the bastinado, the sword, and the bowstring? But the children of Soudan never forgot their own pure religion, though they bent beneath the yoke of the tyrant. Even under the iron rule of the Viceroys of the Porte, we were suffered to sacrifice to Sidi-Belal at the Feast of Beans on the shore of the sea, and to the Djins at the Ayoun-Beni-Menad. Do you not recognise proofs in this of righteousness and truth?"

"Doubtless it is most remarkable," answered Azzahra; "and customs of such venerable antiquity cannot fail to command, at least, our reverential respect. Although the blessed Koran clearly enjoins homage to Allah alone, I can no longer deny that my mind begins slightly to waver. Good and evil spirits, as your creed maintains, may perchance exert some supernatural influence over the affairs and the destinies of man. But how does it happen, Kredoudja," she went on, "that these pagan rites of yours are never attended by a single Mahometan or Jewish man, though so many women of both creeds partake with avidity in the solemn ceremonies? I hear that this is the invariable custom, and that such is the case I plainly perceived at the Ayoun-Beni-Menad, where not a single man was present save those of your own race, and those few were the hired musicians."

"You know that in all religious persuasions the women are more devout than the men," the other replied in a tone of authority which disarmed further criticism. "Were it otherwise, and were the women as indifferent as the other sex in spiritual matters, the priests would drive but a sorry trade. Even in the Christian temples of our conquerors how small is the attendance of the men!"

Kredoudja's scruples as to the risks likely to be incurred in attending the Derdeba were easily overcome by the enthusiastic ardour of her young mistress, and it was arranged that at dusk they were to set out upon their secret expedition.

While they were talking they heard some one creeping cautiously along the balcony, with the intention, as they believed, of overhearing their conversation.

But they were needlessly alarmed. It was but Selim Mustapha returning to inquire after his child. Finding her still depressed, he insisted on her accompanying him on foot along the shore, that the sea-breeze might revive her and restore her drooping spirits. Azzahra was forced to submit, for it was vain to contend against his iron will, though she longed to be left alone with her sorrows until the night should come.

The passing glimpse she caught of Henry, as he swept past her at the gate of the Jardin d'Essai, opened her bleeding wounds afresh, and gave a renewed shock to her already shattered nerves; but she mastered her feelings so as to hide the inward struggle from the eyes of her companion.

As soon as they returned home Azzahra pleaded fatigue and exhaustion, and she prayed her father to leave her that she might seek the refreshment of sleep, for she dreaded that ill-timed anxiety for her welfare might keep him by her side until past the hour for the Derdeba.

Unsuspicious of guile or malice the doting parent willingly complied, believing that she required rest; but, when departing, he told her he would return later to pass the evening in her company, and describe for her entertainment the wild scenes of desert life in which she was about to mingle.

"Lie down now, my beloved child, and take your repose," he affectionately said, kissing her cheek. "It sorely grieves me to see you thus worn out by excitement. To-night I must strive hard to cheer you up."

A few days before this tender solicitude would have been deemed a heaven-sent boon ; now it was considered an intrusion and an annoyance. Such returns for unrequited affection must man look for here below. He lavishes his love upon a stone, and marvels to find it cold and lifeless to his touch. He believes in woman, and wonders that she betrays.

No sooner had he departed than Azzahra sprang from the couch where she had been reclining in feigned exhaustion, and called aloud for her attendant.

"Pity me, Kredoudja!" she exclaimed, narrating what had taken place. "What is to be done now, for to attend the Derdeba is impossible?"

"Leave all to me," replied Kredoudja mysteriously, as she hastened from the apartment.·

Shortly she returned with another Negress, a hideous withered old woman.

"This is a sorceress," said Kredoudja to her mistress, "who is learned at divining by palmistry, and in whose knowledge and skill great confidence is felt. She will read your fortune unfailingly."

Much against Azzahra's will, the hag took hold of her delicate hand, surveying long the lines within the palm.

"Your love will be happy and blessed," at length exclaimed the crone; "but beware of a fair woman who will cross your path!"

"When may I look for that danger to come?" asked Azzahra, interested in this spirit of divination. "When will this fair woman cross my path?"

"She is crossing your path now," answered the other with a fiendish leer, and a grin on her toothless mouth.

"But shall I not triumph?" demanded her dupe. "Even now you told me how my love would be happy and blessed."

"You will triumph in the end," rejoined the soothsayer, "but not till after many days of sorrow and despair. Go your ways, meanwhile; you will meet your lover where you least expect."

CHAPTER XII.

A GLEAM OF SUNSHINE.

BROODING over his enforced separation from Azzahra rendered Wilton so restless and unhappy that he pined for occupation to relieve his troubled thoughts.

Therefore, although expecting but indifferent sport (as all the best ground is preserved), he arranged for a shooting expedition on the Metidja Plains with Frederick Somerton, Olinda's young brother, who had lately arrived.

Instead of thus seeking to put Azzahra for the moment from his thoughts, a lover more enthusiastic, more unreasoning than himself would have at once attacked the fortress where he had discovered the object of his affections, and would perhaps have carried away the prize. But in Henry's mind prudent thoughtful anxiety for the fair name of Azzahra was uppermost He hesitated to approach the spot again too soon lest suspicion might be aroused.

So it happened that he over-diplomatised, for

when he determined to commence it was already too late—Azzahra had left.

But this he knew not. He believed the fruit was waiting ready to be plucked off the stem ; he believed the delay had been prudent, and had probably prevented him from rushing into unseen difficulties and dangers.

Although Azzahra had departed, however, Fortune favoured their meeting, albeit but for a moment, in a way he could never have anticipated.

As Wilton and Frederick drove down the Sahel heights towards the Metidja through woods and rocky dells, the splendid landscape lay before them of the great plain, bounded in the far distance by the vast snowy semicircle of the Atlas, and studded with rising French colonies that nestled in groups of trees surrounded by smiling fields.

The cousins, alighting, traversed a large extent of scrub-clad heights, long grass, and sedgy swamps, likely ground apparently for game, but without success.

Presently they came to a thick tangled growth of tall reeds and brushwood, and forced their way through the dense mass, having heard that the grassy mounds inside afforded good cover for game. But no sooner had they entered than, in their efforts to push on, they plunged headlong into large deep hollows filled with water that lay between the knolls.

Deep were the ejaculations of disgust and
rage that escaped their lips as they floundered
about in the swamp. But their labours and
disappointments were destined to be rewarded
after all, and that in a manner most unexpected.

There happened to be a boar-hunt that day on
the adjacent hills of the Sahel, and one of the
wild-boars driven down from above by the
hunters was charging across the open country
for the cover of the gigantic reeds where the
cousins were scrambling out of the water, the
shelter of the higher ground inside being often
sought by these animals.

The shouts of their *cocher* on the road above
brought out Henry and Frederick just in time to
have a shot each at the boar as he dashed past,
and to roll him over—a feat at which they greatly
rejoiced, having made up their minds for a
blank day.

After killing the boar they ascended to the
highroad, to take charge of the horses and carriage while the caléche-driver was carrying up
their spoil. But the animal was too heavy for
one man to drag up the hill alone, so Frederick
was running back to assist him, when he
saw a man dressed as a mendicant Marabout
approaching, accompanied by two women
closely veiled, and by a greyhound covered with
scars where he had been gored by wild-boars'

tusks. He called out to this man and offered him a franc to go down and help in getting up the boar, which the other, after a few moments' reflection, accepted with cringing humility.

Scarce had the seeming beggar descended a few steps when, at a sign from one of the women, the other unveiled, and Henry instantly recognised the face of Kredoudja.

Her companion, though veiled, he of course knew must be his Azzahra, and he lost not a moment in springing to her side. A dwarf lentisk-bush intervened between them and the men gone to fetch the boar, so their movements could not be observed. He seized the opportunity to beseech her to unveil once more that he might gaze on her loved face; and no sooner had she granted the request than he imprinted impassioned kisses upon her smiling lips, while Frederick and Kredoudja, with commendable prudence, pretended to be deeply occupied in watching the men below.

" Oh, what joy! what bliss! my darling girl," he fervently exclaimed, " to see you once more after I thought you were lost to me for ever!— to hold sweet converse with you thus, and to clasp you in my arms! But why here in this humble guise? Why journey on foot, and in company with this common man? Oh! for

Heaven's sake speak, and solve the unaccountable mystery!"

"You do not then recognise my father," she said in reply, "of whose hospitality you partook the day you were at our house?"

"He is so disguised," Wilton replied, "that no one could possibly discover his identity."

"Of course not," said Azzahra; "discovery would be ruin."

"Wherefore, though, is he clothed in beggar's attire, and wherefore does he perform for me this menial office?"

"For weighty reasons," she whispered in reply. "We are leaving Algiers for the distant Oases of the Sahara, and he seeks to elude the vigilance of the police, who have strict orders to watch his movements. As we were coming out of the town a known spy passed us, and we are terrified lest he should have perceived us and be following in pursuit. Even now a figure glided through the *broussaille* by the roadside, and my father hopes to disarm suspicion, should we be tracked, by pretending to enact his assumed part of a mendicant in· accepting your money."

"How galling must be this degradation!" he continued. "I noticed the proud spirit of your father the last day I saw you, my sweet love, when they carried you away and I dared not follow."

"He knows it is but for a moment," she answered, "and that joy will come on the morrow. At the foot of this hill our mules and attendants await our coming."

"Heaven be praised," passionately exclaimed Henry, "that I have at last discovered whither you are bound! I will follow in your footsteps, were it to the farthest end of the world, so that I may ever be close to your side."

"Alas! this is impossible," she sorrowfully interrupted. "Your life, and perhaps mine, would pay the forfeit did Selim Mustapha suspect that his child even held converse with a Christian."

"Then fly with me this moment!" he cried in despair. "Let us live for each other—be all the world to each other!"

"How could I leave my dear good father, who so fondly loves me and is so kind to me?" she mournfully pleaded, looking lovingly in his eyes.

"But our Christian religion enjoins that man and wife should give up father and mother, and should cleave together; so you would do no wrong in leaving your father with me—that is, if you love me and wish to share my lot for life."

In his suddenly awakened transport of passionate love marriage was the uppermost thought. Position, fortune, family, all he would give up so that he might possess her. Reason and reflection were for the time annihilated within.

"I know that is written in your Great Book," she said, deeply blushing.

"How can you know that?" he inquired in amazement. "Have not you been reared in the faith of the Mahometans?"

"So my father believes," she replied; "but I have been taught besides the beautiful doctrines of the Christians."

"Did not my heart tell me aright the first moment I saw you!" he cried in delight. "I knew well you resembled not the insipid inanimate women of these lands."

"Heaven forbid!" she sighed. "Sad indeed would be my lot were I not superior to those heartless, soulless beings!"

"Oh! what a treasure have I found! And am I to lose you now so soon again, my adored Azzahra?" he groaned. "The sorrow will be greater than I can bear. Oh! say you will be mine! Say you will fly away with me now! Does not the strange manner in which we have met thus for the third time prove that we are destined for each other?"

"That I believe," she artlessly ejaculated, "for a Negress who told my fortune assured me that our love would triumph, and that we should meet far away from here."

Henry could scarcely repress a smile at her innocent credulity and earnestness.

"Surely that would seem to indicate," he said, embracing her, "that I should follow you in your journeyings to the South?"

This argument appeared to have great weight, but after a few seconds' reflection she replied:

"No, no—I durst not; the risk would be too great. But in two or three moons I shall be again in Algiers. Will you give me your sacred promise not to return before then to Europe? Once I come back, Kredoudja will contrive to find us ample opportunities of meeting."

"Ah! but your father may detain you in the desert. How can you undertake to speak with certainty of his movements when you well know the reckless enterprises in which he is ever engaged?"

"What mean you?" she shrieked, terrified. "In mercy speak, and say what you have heard —say to what you allude!"

"Your secret is safe in my keeping," he answered, softly caressing her. "But, I would ask, is it right that a gentle delicate female should take part in deeds of strife, perhaps of blood, such as you will be sure to witness? You know this is not woman's mission; you know you should keep aloof from such scenes."

This was a trying ordeal, for her heart hankered after the wild excitement of Bedouin life, with its dangers and even its lawlessness. Yet, on the other hand, her love urged her to conform to Henry's European ideas, and to abandon her project.

Seeing her hesitate, he eagerly continued:

"Oh, relinquish such an unwomanly life! Come with me, dearest, to Europe, where you will be honoured and loved—where your gentle feminine attributes will be appreciated—where your beauty will be adored—where you will find happiness and rest. There is yet time. Once in yonder coppice your father could not overtake us, and we should be free!"

A gentle fond pressure on his arm told him the fortress had surrendered, and that she was his.

Glancing through the group of lentisks he saw that Selim Mustapha and the *cocher*, bearing the boar between them, were close at hand, and, seizing Azzahra in his arms, he hurried off towards the adjoining copse.

But Kredoudja rushed forward to stop them.

"It is too late," she screamed, catching hold of Azzahra; "escape is now impossible. Your father cannot fail to see you flying and to overtake you. With his temper and his abhorrence of the Christians you can foresee the result."

Kredoudja pointed to where Selim Mustapha was struggling round the end of the brushwood, and Azzahra had only a moment, before veiling again, to let her lover give her one more parting embrace.

"Adieu!" she sighed, weeping bitterly, as she hurriedly covered her face. "Remember your loving broken-hearted Azzahra when she is far, far away."

Wilton was forced to forego the reiteration of his vows in response, for Selim Mustapha was close at hand. There was barely time as she left to make her promise to show a white handkerchief in her window as a signal when she returned to Algiers.

"I promise," she hurriedly answered. "Farewell!"

"You shot that boar well," Selim Mustapha called out, breathless from toiling up the hill with his heavy load. "Though you see me so meanly dressed to-day you can perceive by the wounds on that dog that I hunt the boar myself at times."

"Without doubt you do," exclaimed a gruff voice in the thicket behind, "when you can spare time from your rebel warfare in the desert."

On hearing this all looked round in surprise, but no one was in sight. As to Selim Mustapha and Azzahra, they appeared petrified with terror, and rapidly descending by the road that led to

Blidah across the Metidja, followed by Kre-doudja, they were soon lost to Wilton's anxious gaze.

As he saw Azzahra vanish from sight his grief and despair were unbounded. Frederick strove hard to rouse him from his reverie, but he prayed to be left alone for a while to try and obtain one more glimpse of Azzahra in the plain beneath as she emerged from the wooded heights. To pass the time, therefore, Frederick took the carriage to a spot where the driver assured him he would get some sport.

No sooner was Wilton alone, seated on a bank by the roadside, than he felt a hand laid on his shoulder.

"You know those people?" said the stranger. "Who are they? What are they? When did you meet them?"

The man was dressed as a Spaniard, and Henry felt angry at his unwarrantable intrusion.

"I decline to answer your questions," he coldly replied, "and I request you will leave. You have no right to interfere with me, or to force yourself into my presence."

"Pardon me," the man interposed in a tone of authority. "Though in Spanish costume, I am an agent of the police; and I have good reason to suspect that the man to whom you have just been speaking is a dangerous rebel, whose movements it is my special duty to watch. All are bound to aid the authorities, and I again call on you to tell what you know about those three persons with whom you seem so intimate. Do they not reside in the Arab quarter of Algiers, and do they not occupy one of the largest mansions there, though now assuming this disguise of poverty?"

"You are exceeding your duty by questioning an Englishman in this way," Wilton haughtily replied. "I again repeat that I shall give you no information."

"Then you do not deny my assertion as to where they live?" the other continued with a fierce scowl. "That is enough for me. It tells me I am on the right track, and that I shall soon have the satisfaction of dragging your friends to the bar of justice."

As the spy entered the thicket again to follow the fugitives, Wilton's anguish was unbounded at the thought of the dangers by which Azzahra was beset. He longed to follow and warn her, but he felt his interference would be both unwise and unavailing.

Oh! what torture not to know the fate of his prized Azzahra!—not to be able to aid her and protect her in her hour of need! Would that Selim Mustapha had stayed away for even five minutes longer! he thought. Would that Kredoudja had let him take his chance of escape with his treasure into the coppice! Would that he had insisted on making the attempt!

His beloved one would now be happy in his arms, safe from the terrible calamities into which her father's treason seemed destined to plunge her.

CHAPTER XIII.

RUN TO GROUND.

"We are followed, Azzahra," exclaimed Selim Mustapha, gasping with terror, as they rapidly descended the hill. "That terrible voice was the voice of the pursuer. Our sole chance of escape is to blind and mislead him by turning sharp to the right, and then striking back up the hill again through the thick cover, after we have gone along the road for some distance. The climb over such rough ground will surely tax your strength, my poor child; but, unless we succeed in this stratagem, we are lost, for to continue straight forward must prove fatal. Though even now our attendants and mules are close by, we must seek safety in the opposite direction. Away in the Tell you will often see that greyhound of mine course a hare, and you will see the hare double nimbly back, escaping, as though by a miracle, at the moment Kara-kouch appears to be clutching it between his teeth. In like manner will we elude this spy, for he must be far behind us yet, or he would be in view on that long extent of road we see."

At the base of the hill the road took a sudden turn to the right, and here Selim Mustapha, beckoning to Azzahra and Kredoudja to follow, dashed rapidly into the thicket, so as to scale the heights before the spy could miss them off the thoroughfare.

But the latter was too wary to be so easily circumvented, and had anticipated such a stratagem. He knew as well as they did that to carry out their purpose they must shape their course to the right along the Sahel, for if they kept to the left, or straight forward, they would soon get out into the open country of the Metidja. So he remained in the copse where he had already followed them for such a long time, merely descending lower towards the part where they would be certain to pass. Here he lay down, concealed behind a bank, and very shortly had the satisfaction of seeing the fugitives hurry along in breathless haste, vainly imagining that they had succeeded in baffling his pursuit.

"Allah be praised, we are safe!" ejaculated Selim Mustapha, as he sat down to rest when he thought all danger of being followed was over."
"Would that I could slay that traitorous spy who ever haunts my steps!"

And a villainous bloodthirsty expression of hatred passed over the face of the rebel, which made Azzahra shudder.

" After what has happened we dare not cross the Tell by Blidah," he went on, "for this accursed Christian dog would not fail to intercept us there. We must continue along the Sahel and strike for the mountains of the Chenoua. Once among those wild fastnesses we can set our pursuers at defiance; they could never find us there."

When Azzahra heard that they were to keep along the Sahel towards the Promontory of Chenoua she was greatly pleased, as she knew their course must lie past the Koubba-er-Roumia, or Tomb of the Christian; for her father had taken her up to the heights of Bou-Zareah to show her the lovely prospect from the top, whence she had wondered at the huge mysterious conical pile far away, as it rose aloft above the sea. For her this ruin possessed much interest, because Madame Lagrange was constantly adducing it as an irrefutable proof that Christianity had of old been the religion of the country.

" Could a doubt exist as to the truth of the tradition that this was erected for the mausoleum of a Christian princess," the Frenchwoman was wont to argue, "it must vanish on seeing the large cross carved in stone above one of the doorways, which demonstrates beyond dispute that it was the work of Christians."

But the worthy lady's bigoted zeal to indoctrinate her pupil led her to a false conclusion.

Though the French have chosen to translate the name "Koubba-er-Roumia" as *Tombeau de la Chrétienne,* the term literally means "Tomb of the Roman," which proves nothing about religion, for the Romans held Africa from the time of Cæsar's conquest, when paganism was the religion of the State. As regards the engraven cross, moreover, it is supposed to have been carved by some devout Roman soldier quartered in the camp which stood close to the Tomb.

Be that as it may, Pomponius Melas, who wrote eighteen hundred years ago, speaks of this monument as being so ancient at that time that its origin was lost in the mists of antiquity; consequently it could have been no Christian erection.

But Azzahra, in her simple faith, believed what her instructress told. Christianity, and all things connected with its pure form of worship, possessed a strange powerful fascination over her mind. She longed to visit the wondrous old pile and examine its venerable remains.

When she told Selim Mustapha how ardently she desired to see the Tomb, he promised to gratify her wish, little suspecting the reason which prompted the request.

"My darling Azzahra!" he continued, putting his arm round her and fondly caressing her, "these fatigues must sorely try you, unused as are your poor delicate limbs to the toils of travel. But cheer up, my child; soon we shall be among the Beni-Menasser in the wilds of the Chenoua. They will provide us with mules for our journey, with attire worthy of our rank, and with all we require."

A loud rustling noise, as of some large body passing quickly through the brushwood close at hand, resounded on their terrified ears, but at the same moment Karakouch crept tremblingly to their feet for protection. They knew therefore some wild animal, probably a jackal or a hyæna, had raised this unwonted alarm, for had a man been so near the dog would have stood at bay to defend them.

After long and weary scrambling through dense brushwood, over projecting rocks, across deep ravines, and along rough stony paths that cruelly pained the tender feet of his companions, he led the way into a *café maure*, first satisfying himself, by cautiously peering over the top of a mound, that they were not followed.

The Quahouadji, or proprietor, was an old acquaintance, in whose house Selim Mustapha had often held rendezvous with his fellow-rebels.

This man he took into his confidence, telling him how the French police had been upon his track, and got him to promise—though with great .reluctance through fear of detection, and only after long persuasion—that he would deny the presence of guests in his house should any suspicious-looking stranger come to make inquiries.

"This you can do with perfect safety," added Selim Mustapha, "as the spy lost all trace at the bottom of the hill where I turned this way through the woods ; for I could see a considerable distance back along the road, and he was not visible. He is sure to be on the look-out for me at Blidah, seeing that I was journeying in that direction, and judging that I would still work thither on my way to the Desert, to join my bands through the gorge of the Chiffa and Medeah."

"Was such your intention, then ? " asked the Quahouadji.

"It would have been hazardous," the other replied, "to continue on such a thoroughfare. After passing Blidah I would have turned to the right by the heights of Mouzaïa across the Djendel country towards Milianah, when I had ascended some distance up the gorge of the Chiffa."

"And reached the South by that route, instead of by Medeah ? " asked the host.

"Yes; I should have kept to the west, and entered the Sahara by Teniet-el-Hâad, as I purpose now," his guest replied.

The Quahouadji complimented Selim Mustapha on the skilful plan he had laid for evading pursuit, and joined in thinking that watch would be kept at Blidah, under the belief that the party would yet follow out what seemed to be their plan of passing that town on the way southward.

"You give praise, oh! trusty friend, for the line of travel I struck out to evade pursuit," whispered Selim Mustapha, a scowl of blood-thirsty fury creeping over his face. "But sometimes pursuit cannot be evaded; then it must be stopped. In the Djendel, Yakoub, none are near to hear or see."

"Masterly splendid plan!" exclaimed Yakoub, surveying his guest with respectful admiration, when he comprehended the hidden meaning. "Wonderful prudence! Of a certainty no eye would witness the deed there, no ear would hear the death-scream. But would you murder before your child?" added Yakoub.

"What would you have?" the other evasively replied, with a meaning shrug of his shoulders. "Besides, the women need not look. They could turn their heads, or move away, while I drove my dagger into the craven's heart."

Selim Mustapha then joined the young

women, and they all retired to an inner room, where they shut themselves up for the rest of the day in close concealment.

At night, finding no one arrived except the native neighbours, who were well known to the Quahouadji, Selim Mustapha emerged from his retirement and joined the group of customers in the outer room. Here, squatted on the ground, they were drinking coffee from small fendjal cups, smoking, and playing at draughts— the squares of the draught-boards being level or hollow alternately, instead of being coloured black and white as on the draught-boards of Europe; while the Quahouadji was busily engaged bruising the coffee-berries in a mortar, preparing the coffee at his stove, and serving it round to his visitors.

"There is no danger at this late hour, my good friend," he said, as Selim Mustapha approached to where he was putting a live coal with a pair of tongs to the pipe of one of the draught-players. "You may join us now without apprehension. A Rami is coming presently who excels in narrating stories—several from the 'Thousand and One Nights,' but he knows many original tales besides. Ah! here he is," he called out, hearing a footstep approach the door; "to-night he comes earlier than usual."

But it was not the Rami, or story-teller, that entered. It was a tall powerful man who, though dressed in the costume of a Spanish bordelais-carrier, was evidently a Frenchman.

He seated himself on a bench that was covered with a mat, and ordered the Quahouadji to serve him with coffee out of a large cup, instead of out of the ordinary fendjal.

"Those miserable little fendjals hold nothing," he said, pushing one aside that stood on the table in its egg-cup-like saucer. "After a man has had a hard day's walk he wants a good drink. But I can see by your *papouches* that none here have journeyed far to-day—except you," he added, pointing to Selim Mustapha's travel-stained slippers. "You seem to have come a long distance."

Although well disguised, Selim Mustapha at once recognised him as the man who always hovered about his house in the Quartier Arabe at Algiers, and whom he had frequently deceived by the different characters he assumed. Now he felt that he had been discovered at last, and that the fellow was quietly tracking him to obtain proofs of his guilt and to entrap his associates. But he concealed his apprehensions, replying that he had travelled that day from the Baths of Hammam R'ira in the Chenoua.

"Then your women of course are with you?" observed the mock Spaniard with a malicious grin. "The natives always take their wives there to pray to Sidi Sliman, the Prince of the Djins."

"They are taken to pray for offspring," the Arab evasively replied. "My wives, Allah be praised! have no need to go."

"Are your women not with you, then?" asked the other in a tone of authority that seemed to demand a reply.

Were it not for the state of alarm in which he had been plunged by the sudden appearance of the spy, Selim Mustapha would have resented bitterly this impertinent curiosity about his women, so offensive to the Oriental; but he simply replied that he was alone.

"Whose then are the female voices I heard even now in that inner room?" the Frenchman continued, giving the Arab a searching look.

"They are my wives," interrupted the Quahouadji, who was as much frightened as his guest, for he dreaded being discovered harbouring rebels.

"Nay, friend, that cannot be true," answered the other with an insolent sneer. "You have but one wife, I know well, and her I saw this moment in that room to the left."

"By the beard of the Prophet, they are the sisters of my wife!" urged the man in great alarm; "but they are very young, and I suffer them not to appear in public, even veiled."

"Be it so, my good man," answered the spy, thinking it better to appear satisfied with this explanation, for he feared he might have excited too much the suspicions of his victim; "I desire not to pry into your private affairs."

The Rami now arrived, and delighted the audience with his recitals. After a long narration from the "Arabian Nights' Entertainments," the Quahouadji requested him to favour the company with a tale of his own composition.

"I will recite 'Zolinda's Bath,'" answered the Rami, "which has been a good deal admired, I am proud to say, and which I trust will merit your approval."

ZOLINDA'S BATH.

Zolinda loved her limbs to lave
Within the cool transparent wave.
Beside a limpid stream she lay
That sparkled ever bright and gay.
The fairest flowers were smiling there,
The rarest scents perfumed the air;
The sweetest sounds of music crept
Around, to soothe her while she slept.
Birds, in the brightest plumage dressed,
Sang sweetly in this bower of rest.
Pure marble glittered on the floor,
Fountains were playing evermore,
And gaily flinging spray around
That wooed the ear with soothing sound.
Pure lilies twined in fairest wreath
Upon the crystal tide beneath.
Bright fish with scales of golden gleam
Disported in that wooing stream.

A silken awning, bright and rare,
Preserved cool freshness in the air,
Shading the burning noontide heat
From this—Zolinda's loved retreat.
No spot she thought so fair as this,
This was her bower of love and bliss.
Fair maidens stood in glittering throng
Prepared to wake the tuneful song.
They fanned her with their punkas oft,
As on her couch, so rich and soft,
She lay with warm lascivious eye,
Blest in this dream of luxury.
Delicious viands, sweets; and fruit
They bore on gold, with noiseless foot.
Her snowy hand lay on her lute,
Bright slippers held her fairy foot.
Her eyebrows rose in arching height
O'er her black eyes of dazzling light.
Her tresses fell in raven flow
Upon a neck of purest snow.
Her nose was of the Grecian form,
Her cheek with roseate tinges warm.
Enchanting smiles, for ever new,
Played round her lips, as though to woo.
Soft plaintive sighs stole from her breast,
She longed—she pined—to be caressed.

"Oh, where is Mustapha?" she sighed.
"How long he lingers from my side!
Would I could gaze upon his face,
And feel his loving warm embrace!
Oh, joy! I hear his footstep sound.
Fly! Lead him to this fairy ground."

Zolinda sighed and hoped in vain.
Never may Mustapha again
Delight those luscious melting eyes—
Never more breathe impassioned sighs.

It was not Mustapha who came;
It was the avenger of her shame,
Mad to take vengeance on his wife
And slay her with his gleaming knife.

He rushed in, wild with rage and hate,
Through the scared maidens at the gate
Zolinda fondly sent to guide
Her favoured lover to her side.
His knitted brows proclaimed his ire,
His eyeballs glared like globes of fire,
His robes bore many a bloody stain :
Whose blood was there ?   Whom had he slain ?

Her outraged lord, with frantic stride—
Bloodthirsty—sought Zolinda's side,
Where the frail beauty trembling knelt,
O'erwhelmed with fear and conscious guilt.
He seized her by her waving hair,
And brandished high his knife in air.

"Base wretch !" with choking voice he cried,
" When you became my cherished bride
I little dreamed you would betray—
Dishonour me, while far away.
In distant lands I heard your shame ;
Though disbelieving, swift I came,
To find, alas ! that hope and trust
Were shattered by a wanton's lust.
As I sprang through yon outer gate,
I met the object of my hate
With stealthy step and smiling face
Coming to bask in your embrace.
I took the coward traitor's life,
I slew him with this trusty knife.
Go, join your lover in the grave !
Polluted, false, unworthy slave ! "

He spake, and struck one deadly blow
Upon her heaving breast of snow ;
Then flung her on the marble floor—
Zolinda's dream of love was o'er !

As soon as the Rami had concluded, the loud
praises of the company showed how deeply they
had enjoyed his recitation, delivered with all the

skill and genius of an Oriental story-teller. Then silence prevailed, for the presence of the stranger cast a shadow of gloom and suspicion on the party. One by one the guests departed, until none were left but Selim Mustapha and the pretended Spaniard.

CHAPTER XIV.

KIF IN A CAFÉ MAURE.

SELIM MUSTAPHA hoped that the spy might have left with the remainder of the company to keep watch outside, and that he should still be able to escape in the darkness of the night; but the man moved not, maintaining a stolid sturdy gaze into the crackling embers of the wood-fire. Then Selim Mustapha plainly saw that his worst suspicions were realised, and that the man was in hot pursuit.

Yet he dared not betray the terror he inwardly felt, as he sat face to face with his persecutor; for he well knew his sole chance of safety lay in putting the other off his guard, making him believe he was unrecognised by his victim.

Assuming, therefore, a careless unconcerned manner, Selim Mustapha called out to the Quahouadji to fetch him a pipeful of *hachish*; and he took out from beneath his burnous his small hachish-pipe, which he commenced to clean out with a pocket-knife and prepare for smoking.

"Bring me hachish also," said the mock Spaniard. "I will join you in your smoke," he added, turning towards Selim Mustapha. "The soothing repose of *kif* will be welcome after my hard fatiguing journey to-day. The ways are rough and tiring through the tangled woods of the Sahel." And he looked steadfastly at Selim Mustapha, as though expecting an answer.

"I know not," said the other, thus appealed to, with an affectation of careless confidence he was far from feeling. "I have never travelled in the Sahel off the beaten tracks. Why, in the name of Allah, seek out rocky and thorny ways, when our conquerors, in their bountiful magnanimity, have graciously provided us with such admirable roads—military roads, to enable them to scour the country from end to end, and thereby keep us in subjection, simply for our own advantage?"

Although thus putting on such a bold independent manner, and using such freedom of speech, the Arab was trembling abjectly at heart; and the moment the host left the room for the pipes of hachish, he followed and threw himself on the man's mercy, explaining how he was hunted down, and imploring his assistance to escape from the meshes of the net with which his enemy was surrounding him.

Selim Mustapha whispered piteously in the ear of the Quahouadji how the fellow had traced them the whole day with the instinctive sagacity

of a bloodhound, following everywhere, like a
shadow, though himself unperceived, and how
his pursuit was so keen that it almost created
despair of eluding such ceaseless vigilance, now
that he was unquestionably on their track.

"Should I fail to circumvent him to-night,"
he went on, pleading for sympathy, " the blood-
stained wretch will never relax his grip until he
drags me to the ground. The sole means of
delivery out of his hand, that I can see, for my
child and myself lies in his becoming stupefied
with the hachish; and towards producing this
result you, my friend Yakoub, can give most
material assistance. Its fumes will speedily
overpower him, for he has travelled far to-day
and is unaccustomed to the use of the drug. On
the morrow, ere he awakes, we shall be far away
in safety."

"Rely on my aid," eagerly responded Yakoub,
whose sympathies, being an Arab, were warmly
enlisted on the side of a fellow-native, especially
when that native was a chieftain in danger
through devotion to his country. " All that lies
in my power I shall gladly do to facilitate your
escape."

But a still stronger incentive to secure the
safe departure of his guests than even patriotism
was the knowledge that on the morrow the
Frenchman would discover that the women in
the inner room were no relatives of his, but were

in company with Selim Mustapha. Then of a surety he would be charged with knowingly harbouring rebels, having concealed the party and denied their presence in his house.

The cordial manner in which Yakoub espoused his cause, and which he attributed solely to sentiments of patriotism and friendship, greatly relieved the mind of Selim Mustapha, for the man's hesitation and evident apprehension at first made him doubt his fidelity.

"We must manage in this wise, Yakoub," he hurriedly continued. "It must be so arranged that the Indian hemp shall stupefy him, but not me; for I shall have to smoke as well, to disarm suspicion. Having been the first to call for hachish, the spy would be at once on his guard were I now to hang back. Besides, his plan may be to try and smoke me down, so as to render me insensible, and therefore safe for the night. If so, he will fall into a trap he little expects."

"How can this be done?" asked the Quahou-adji, looking sceptically at his guest.

"What I want you to do," the other replied, "is to fill this man's pipe with hachish, putting only ordinary tobacco in mine. Suspecting nothing, he will be easily led on to surrender himself a helpless victim into our hands. Once under the influence of kif, I could set the Christian dog at defiance and free myself from his grasp. Oh! that while he lies buried in the sleep of stupefaction Azzahra and I may get clear from the toils he has spread! Then, Yakoub, my faithful and long-tried friend, I can rely on you to afford me this much-needed assistance?" continued Selim Mustapha.

"Ay, and much more, to extricate you from this great peril that threatens your very existence," the Quahouadji warmly responded. "My heart is with you and your brave band of comrades, who, with the blessing of Allah, will yet fulfil our ancient prophecy of driving the tyrant oppressor into the sea at the Oued Isser. Base indeed should I prove myself did I not help you in your hour of need, after you have been so often my guest, and after you have so often brought your warrior companions hither to honour my humble abode. Yet be not too sanguine, Selim Mustapha, in your hope to baffle and outwit the French spy. Fortune and honour would be his could he succeed in identifying you as the great conquering Chieftain of the Desert. Easier would it be to turn aside the lion in his spring through the air than to divert this man from his deadly purpose. Indulge not the hope, then, O friend of my bosom! that he will suffer his senses to be stolen from him by the leaf of the Indian hemp while he is in pursuit of such coveted game. But we will try, my brother—we will try; and Allah grant in his mercy that we may succeed!

In you I see the last chance for my poor down-trodden country to throw off the yoke of the usurper. With you a prisoner, she may well despair of her lot and fling hope to the winds."

"Fear not, good Yakoub," said Selim in reply, laying his hand upon the shoulder of his host. "Heaven will favour our enterprise, and I shall outwit him. Then, when once free from the base traitor, he shall never more cross my path."

"What mean you?" demanded the Quahouadji, in alarm. "You do not surely purpose to compass his death?"

"Ask me not," Selim Mustapha replied in a tone of authority. "I will but do what is right, and mete out even-handed justice. As he and his false crew measure unto us, so shall it be measured to them again."

"But you will not kill him in the humble abode of your trusty devoted friend, to bring down destruction on this poor household?' Yakoub piteously groaned, by no means reassured after his guest's explanatory remarks. "In pity take him anywhere else to slay him, and I will gladly lend a helping hand. But I implore of you not to drag me down to ruin and despair by committing this deed of blood under my roof. It will come to light of a surety, Selim Mustapha, and then what will become of me and mine? Oh, think of our long friendship!—think of the years we have been as brothers!—and then have compassion. Bring not on me this terrible disaster, to turn me into a wretched abject coward for life. How could I ever refrain afterwards from a shudder of terror at every stranger who crossed my threshold, knowing that such a hideous crime might at any moment be discovered and laid to my charge?"

"Rest in peace, O friend of my heart!" replied his guest. "No harm shall happen through me to you or yours; not a hair of your heads shall be injured."

All being arranged for putting in force his plans of meditated treachery and vengeance, Selim Mustapha returned and calmly took his seat on the floor beside his enemy, fearing that longer absence might awaken unfavourable comments.

It was to be a trial of skill and patience between these two men as to which of them should outmanœuvre and defeat the other, and each relied confidently on the intoxication of kif for effecting his purpose.

The Frenchman commenced operations at once by pretending to puff vigorously at his pipe, but while displaying such apparent energy he inhaled little of the treacherous stupefying fumes. He sat rocking his body in his chair, his eyes intently fixed upon his companion beneath on the floor, anxiously awaiting the moment when

kif should plunge the smoker into oblivious
slumbers. Then he could without risk, he
thought, snatch a few hours' repose while the un-
believing dog lay stretched senseless at his feet.

What good fortune, he thought, that the
fellow had not recognised him, though having
seen him such scores of times hanging about the
Quartier Arabe that his face ought to be familiar!—that very day even he had passed close to
Selim Mustapha and his women as they were
leaving the city. What good fortune that he
had hidden his movements so skilfully all day
through the Sahel!—once only giving an opportunity for a fleeting glance as he glided from one
patch of cover to another, and this the fugitives
would probably be too preoccupied to notice.
What good fortune that he had so scared them by
his denunciation from out the bushes that they
kept to the woods of the Sahel, where he could
pursue unseen, forsaking their course to Blidah
across the Metidja, on whose open spaces his
every movement would be watched and observed!
What a master-stroke! he thought with pride.
How helplessly, blindly the fools had fallen into
the trap he laid with such consummate skill!

Once or twice he fancied his quarry gave him
an anxious scrutinising glance, but by the way
in which he spoke afterwards Selim Mustapha
removed all fears of recognition. Besides, did
the slightest suspicion exist, would he be guilty of

such monstrous folly as to meddle with hachish? It would be little short of madness.

"Aha! when the poor sot falls down, wrapt in the beatific visions of his kif," the Frenchman silently said to himself in exultation, "he shall have my blessing for sparing me the annoyance and fatigue of keeping watch all night, when I am tired to death already."

He ceased not to marvel how the two young women trudged all day over the rocks and brambles of that accursed *broussaille*, and the rapid pace they went, with which he could barely keep up, having so frequently to creep along the ground and stoop his body for concealment.

"But success has been mine, beyond my most sanguine expectations," he continued, apostrophizing himself. "You will rise to greatness yet, Jean Jacquard, and yonder contemptible robber of the Desert shall supply the ladder by which you will proudly mount the lofty heights of wealth and fame!"

Thus Jean Jacquard communed within himself in the boastful spirit of his class, enjoying already in anticipation the fruits of his forthcoming triumph. He prided himself, and with good reason, on his well-known power of resisting the intoxicating influence of hachish; for, in consequence of this valuable gift, he was always selected by his superior officers for conducting difficult cases that required espionage in the

cafés maures. At these establishments the
golden rule holds good of doing in Rome as the
Romans do. A man who enters there must
smoke hachish like the rest, or be branded as a
dangerous treacherous intruder before whom all
mouths should be dumb.

Relying, therefore, on this his peculiar *spécial-
ité,* he felt confident of reducing his fellow-
smoker before long to a helpless condition of
degraded insensate imbecility. `Great then was
his astonishment at hearing his expected victim
demand from Yakoub a fresh pipe of hachish.

"And mind you make it stronger than the
last," Selim added, angrily addressing the host.
"These rascally Quahouadjis adulterate hachish
now with rubbish so that one can hardly ever
meet it pure," he continued, turning towards the
Frenchman, " and it takes half the night to get
kif."

His companion cast over a look of bitter disappointed rage, but made no comment, though
the inhaling powers of the Arab filled him with
intense surprise and vexation.

"You smoke slowly, friend," Selim Mustapha
went on, taking a goodly whiff at his pipe.
"Why, positively, you have not finished your
first pipe yet, and here am I hard at work with
my second."

"I choose to smoke slowly," the other answered with an angry growl, for he was enraged

at Selim Mustapha's remark. "The habit, I find, often gives me a considerable advantage."

"Keep that habit," the other slowly spluttered forth, feigning to assume the vacant stare and the thick inarticulate speech of the drivelling victim to hachish. "I charge you keep it. Lose not your advantage. It is so hard to get an advantage, and when you have got it keep it. Mark my words, my good friend—mark my words! Haste, give me kif at once, that I may the sooner enjoy the soothing peace it brings, the delectable visions of happiness and rest—oh! such delicious forgetfulness of life and its cares!—such dazzling insights into the unknown and the beautiful! But smoke slowly on—slowly—slowly! You are right. The greater will be your enjoyment. Oh, what joyous delight!" he continued to mutter inarticulately. "This indeed is heavenly bliss!"

He feigned intoxication, because he could clearly perceive the hachish beginning already to take effect on the Frenchman. He knew the moment was drawing nigh to put his project into execution, for he saw the deep part the spy was playing would end in his own discomfiture.

The trap laid by himself he now knew would succeed. He knew that directly he seemed to succumb, and that the excitement of watching his movements ceased, his foe would yield himself up a helpless ready victim to the treacherous narcotic, exhausted as he was by the fatigue of his journey.

After a few more inhalations, therefore, from his fresh pipeful, he displayed all the outward symptoms of kif, to the unspeakable delight and relief of the spy, who previously began to fear that he had met more than his match at last.

A calm tranquil expression of stupor settled upon Selim Mustapha's features, and in a few minutes more he lay extended at full length on the floor, to all appearance in a state of imbecile insensibility.

"It is well," ejaculated the Frenchman, after carefully examining the prostrate figure. "His weary trudge through the wilds of the Sahel will make him repose long and soundly."

A loud deep-drawn snore confirmed his hopes.

"Yes, he is safe till the morning," muttered Jacquard with a grim smile, stretching himself on the ground in front of the fire opposite to his intended victim. "It will be many hours before the effect of this disappears, and in the mean-time my prey is safe. Still over-confidence is unwise. I will indulge in kif, but I will not smoke deeply, for how can I tell what might occur whilst I slept to mar the success of my triumph? Fugitives are proverbially shy and wary. They slip through one's fingers when apparently most off their guard, and Quahouadjis are all contemptible traitors at heart. I will inhale only a little, just sufficient to give me a refreshing sleep after the fatigues of the day, and to prepare me for renewing the pursuit on the morrow. Heaven defend me from imitating this contemptible sot, who for the sake of a transient gleam of happiness loses his liberty and, it may be, his life!

"Oh! what a curse to humanity is this vile habit of the degraded native—one, too, which even his betters are but too prone to acquire! Wherefore did not their impostor Prophet forbid his followers to indulge in this hateful degrading vice when he commanded them to abstain from intoxicating drinks? Surely no drunkenness is so ruinous, so brutalising, so despicable as this! None so stultifies the brain—so debilitates the nerves—so shatters the health—so destroys the intellect! Never will Jean Jacquard bend under its accursed influence! No—no! I have more wit than to turn myself into a drivelling dotard. Yet, oh! how glorious is this kif! what heavenly ecstasy! and I should awake long before that besotted fool. He will sleep the sleep of the blessed, and the Quahouadji will not dare to play me false—me? Jean Jacquard?" he added, proudly smiting his hand upon his breast. "But, stay, what am I saying? He knows not I am Jean Jacquard; what matters? All will go right —yes, yes, all will go right—and I must take some sleep.

"I will only indulge this once—never, never again, I swear—I solemnly swear. Oh! fool—idiot that I am! Why can I not resist, now that such brilliant prospects open out before me? Yes, I feel I shall be known to fame! I shall found my fortune through this contemptible hog, who never before did a good action, nor conferred benefit on mortal. I see it all mapped out as clear and distinct as the light of day. Jean Jacquard, you will be a great man before you die—a very great man—mark my words! But, oh! I feel so weary—so very weary, I long so to be at rest!"

Thus he babbled on in rambling, disconnected, contradictory outbursts, the sure precursors of the conquering kif. By this disjointed fallacious course of argument he reconciled to his already half-clouded intellect the insensate folly he was about to commit—folly that was not merely to dash to the ground the bright hopes of reward and renown he had so long cherished, but that was likewise to end in a sudden and cruel death.

Oblivious of danger and fame and gain, and of every other sublunary consideration, Jacquard smoked with renewed vigour at his pipe of hachish as he lay upon the floor. Soon he laid down his head and gave himself over to the raptures of kif, with its entrancing visions of boundless enjoyment.

Rightly had Selim Mustapha judged. His foe, he shrewdly reasoned, would readily fall a prey to kif after his toilsome clambering along the Sahel heights, for a European must be more easily affected by the hachish than a man who indulged from childhood in its use.

The sleep of the Frenchman was clearly not feigned, as was his. It was genuine, and he determined it should be long—that it should change into the cold endless sleep of death!

CHAPTER XV.

DEATH OF THE SPY.

CAUTIOUSLY rising, so as not to disturb the prostrate form beside him, Selim Mustapha crept round the room, searching by the dim flicker of the slowly expiring embers on the hearth for a box of carpenter's tools he had noticed on his arrival in the hands of the Quahouadji. He took out a long strong nail and a hammer, and stealthily retraced his steps to where his victim lay, sleeping his last sleep. Pressing the point of the nail softly against the Frenchman's temple he gave it a smart blow with the hammer, driving it home into the skull up to the head.

A slight quivering passed over the body for a few seconds, and then all was still. The spy's ambitious visions of distinction and greatness were ruthlessly dispelled by the icy hand of death. Over him stood the murderer, exulting in his deed of blood, and contemptuously spurning with his foot the lifeless corpse.

The silent pressure of a hand upon his shoulder made him spring round in alarm. The Quahou-adji confronted him, who had heard the heavy blow of the hammer, and came forth suspecting mischief.

"Fear nothing," he whispered; "I will not betray you. But why, oh why, did you kill this man in my house? Why have me suspected and watched for the remainder of my days? Selim Mustapha, you have brought on me and on my house misery and despair."

"Could I have done otherwise? He was hunting me down," expostulated his friend, thinking only of his own misfortunes, while ignoring those he might be bringing on his old companion Yakoub. "Why did he continue to dog my steps, after I gave him one chance for his life? When he was following through the coppice in the Sahel I had but to lie in wait for him in the bushes, instead of flying before him, and stab him with this dagger to the heart."

And he took out from the belt round his waist a long broad knife with an ivory handle in a silver-gilt scabbard of elaborate workmanship.

"That would, of a truth, be an effectual cure for impertinent interference," Yakoub replied, admiring the weapon with the air and eye of a connoisseur. "Would to Heaven you had killed the traitor there, instead of in my lowly house!"

"At that time I wanted not to kill him," said

his guest. "Believe me it is wiser not to murder unless compelled for some good and sufficient reason, as has been my case to-night, for the danger of being found out ever hangs like a sword suspended over one's head. In olden times we could rid ourselves of an enemy without incurring much danger of retributive justice in case of detection. But since these hated Franks have come and taken possession of our land it is as much as one's life is worth to kill a man."

"That is just what I say," groaned Yakoub. "Oh! would that you had murdered this man anywhere but in my wretched struggling coffee-house! Oh! Selim Mustapha, you spoke wisely when you said it is unwise to murder—at least so near Algiers. Away in the interior of the country the police are scarce as yet, Allah be praised, and our taskmasters have not made such encroachments on the liberty of the subject."

"Quite right, Yakoub, and my reason for sparing the wretch this morning was the fear of some one witnessing me strike him to the ground," answered Selim Mustapha. "Now I can kick him—thus," he continued, again spurning the body with his foot. "I tried my utmost to get away and to keep my hands clear of blood, but the perverse madman would persist in rushing to his doom!"

"You should have taken his life in the wood," Yakoub gasped, wringing his hands in the agony of despair; "you should have taken his life in the wood!"

"No, Yakoub; it is unsafe to kill in the woods by day, for a man mortally stabbed will at times give a dying shriek that may echo afar, and bring down the feet of the avenger. Besides, my child was present, and I would not willingly have her witness the shedding of blood, so long as a chance remained for escape."

"But should your daughter see this dead man on the morrow," interposed the Quahouadji, trembling with unreasoning terror, "well will she know how he came by his death, and will peradventure betray us with her heedless babbling woman's tongue. Oh! wretched man that I am!" And he wrung his hands in despair.

"Abject coward! muddle-pated wittol!" Selim Mustapha contemptuously replied. "She see this carrion, think you? How? Will you, forsooth, take and show it her? You reason not, Yakoub; craven terror blinds you, and makes you shudder with fear when no danger exists."

"But I tell you there is danger—very great danger—so long as that vile heap of flesh lies rotting in my house," Yakoub continued to groan. "Oh! should any come and find that terrible nail!—woe is me! woe is me!"

"Look, good Yakoub," interrupted his guest,

endeavouring to allay his fears. "I just arrange the thick curly locks—so—over the top of the nail, which I have beaten down so far into the bone of the skull that the flesh has closed above it. None will ever be the wiser of how he died, mark my words. You perceive too, Yakoub, my precaution of driving the nail at the back, lest some prying meddling fool might discover it while examining the front of the head. Cheer up, and be of good heart, oh! friend of my youth. Fear naught; harm shall not come nigh you. Should questions ever be asked, all you know is that the man came in late and lay down to rest; in the morning he was dead. The will of Allah be done!"

"Were one of our race found murdered, I grant the Government would trouble little with inquiries," replied Yakoub; "but this man is well known by the authorities to be perpetually engaged in searching out treason amongst us, and his sudden death here, in a house known to be frequented solely by natives, cannot fail to excite suspicion. Do you tell me that the body will not be searchingly examined to discover the cause of death? Not a spot but what will be subjected to a rigid scrutiny by the surgeons. Then if that nail be detected, what will become of me, ill-fated wretch that I am? I shall be lost—undone—dragged to prison and, it may be, to the scaffold!"

"Utter not such drivelling nonsense, Yakoub," ejaculated Selim Mustapha, with a smile of ineffable scorn at the pitiable dismay of his companion. "The Bureau Arabe would simply levy a fine on the Kaïd, whom the district would have to reimburse, after which the whole affair which so grievously terrifies you would soon blow over and be forgotten. You have had no quarrel with him—you owe him no grudge. How then could the deed be brought home to you?"

"That may be," returned the Quahouadji; "but they would know I could not be ignorant of who was the murderer, and I am not going to run the chance of detection. Bitterly should I regret being forced to betray the brave chief to whom I look as the future saviour of my country; yet candidly I confess that were I arrested I should without hesitation declare who had committed the crime, that I might screen myself from suspicion. No—no, Selim Mustapha; we will make away with this dead body—we will bury it."

"The foul Christian vermin shall have no burial at my hands, by the tomb of the Prophet!" exclaimed the murderer. "We will remove him hence, as you desire, but his carcass shall be flung out as food for the hyenas and the jackals. Let us carry him down the hill where the thicket is densest, and the wild beasts of the field will soon destroy all trace of his identity, should this carcass ever be found again."

"You advise well," said Yakoub, "for a grave cannot be dug without noise, which in the stillness of the night might be heard by those we should little care to catch us at work."

"True," joined in the other; "we must run no such risk."

"Wonderful, inimitable contrivance! Amazing discovery!" ejaculated the host, lost in profound admiration at this new mode of committing murder, as he felt for the wound on the victim's head. "Positively I can scarce find the place. Is this your own idea?" he resumed, after again examining minutely the ghastly spot.

"Mine, altogether," replied the other, flattered highly at such encomiums on his diabolical invention, though sorely bewailing that it should be thrown away in this case without the honour of public recognition. "And such faith have I in its virtue that I anticipate not the possibility of detection. Still you are right; it is more prudent to conceal the corpse."

"An admirable spot for putting him away safe lies not more than a couple of hundred yards hence," the Quahouadji cautiously whispered, "where a hollow recess has been scooped out by the waters under the bank of an Oued, surrounded by a dense coppice of lentisks and

oleanders. There will we fling him down, and
he will never be seen more save by the wild
beasts of the field."

Then the two proceeded to strip the body, for
the purpose of carefully burying the clothes at
their leisure, so as to destroy all evidence of the
crime. A large signet-ring of gold they took off
likewise, but another ring of galvanised lead
was so deeply imbedded in the flesh that they
allowed it to remain, agreeing that anything so
common could never lead to identification.

" Besides," added Selim, " if we cut off the
finger for the sake of securing this trumpery
ring we shall be certain to shed blood, and
probably mark our burnouses ; whereas now
we can carry this lump of carrion away without
receiving the smallest stain."

" That is what I applaud so highly in your
most ingenious device," Yakoub responded, rub-
bing his hands in rapturous admiration. " Oh,
it is a splendid invention ! Would that I had
known of this in the days of my youth ! Now,
alas ! I am too old, and I lead too indolent a
life to embark in wild adventures."

" And you live in too civilised a part of the
country," added Selim Mustapha. " Were you
along with our band in the far Oases of the
South, you could do anything you chose with a
certainty of impunity."

" What a glorious life ! " sighed Yakoub.

"It is a glorious life," enthusiastically echoed Selim Mustapha. "It is glorious to be free and unfettered. It is glorious to feel you are fighting for the deliverance of your native land from the hand of the stranger. But we are wasting precious time. Let us away with this foul heap of rubbish."

Carrying the body between them, for they feared to drag it along lest a mark might be left upon the ground, they soon reached the spot named by Yakoub. Here, pushing through the thickly growing oleanders that fringed the river-bed, they deposited their ghastly burden, so judiciously concealed that its discovery seemed impossible.

"Ha—ha! The jackals and hyenas are beginning to howl already," laughed Selim Mustapha, with a hearty chuckle of delight, as the loud yelping of the beasts of prey resounded close at hand through the densely tangled oleander and dwarf caroubier scrub along the course of the Oued. "They will soon be at him, gnawing his flesh and crunching his bones. After their banquet is concluded there will be little danger of his being ever identified again, though all the police in Algiers should come to examine his carcass."

CHAPTER XVI.

OVER THE BAY.

THE stormy weather that had prevented the projected water-party to Rusgunia in Edwardes's yacht at length cleared away, and on a bright sunny morning his guests rowed out to the Atlanta, that lay swinging lazily at her moorings in the spacious harbour of Algiers.

The surface of the water was so smooth and unruffled that the ladies clambered with little difficulty from the small rowing-boat on board the yacht, with the exception of Miss Thornton, who furnished great amusement by the prudish care she took to prevent the boatmen beneath from seeing her ankles—a calamity she appeared to regard with profound maidenly horror, though noted for allowing beholders of her own rank in life free scope to study and admire those attractive portions of her person.

The anchor was soon weighed, the sails set, and the helm put down. A light breeze came from the north-west, before which the cutter bounded away and glided over the waves.

For some days Olinda and Henry had both reflected much on their converse in the Jardin d'Essai.

Olinda had hoped that, notwithstanding her cousin's unreasoning advocacy and championship, his faith in Azzahra might be shaken by reflection. But vain was the expectation. His unquestioning passion for the Arabian remained as strong as ever. So did the persuasion that she would cast no discredit on his name—that was to say, should he really decide on making her his bride. This qualifying proviso he always added parenthetically, even in his wildest transports of love, for his mind continued still hazy and undetermined as to whither he was drifting. Putting away, however, all care for the future, he gave free rein to the romantic rapture of the present. Doubts he scattered to the winds, regarding them as little short of sacrilege. Loving as he did, he wished to think his idol perfect, and the wish was father to the thought.

Olinda could plainly detect the current of his reflections by his dejection and silence. She saw he was so love-stricken that argument seemed but to strengthen his resolve and intensify his mad passion. Wherefore she determined to be his mentor no longer, nor seek to sway his actions. The thankless task rendered her miserable, and conferred no benefit upon him. Far, indeed, from proving beneficial, intermeddling tended manifestly to irritate and drive him into angry hostility against herself.

Yet it gave her a bitter pang to withdraw and leave him to his fate—to desert him in his hour of sorest need. She mourned over his coming doom, for she loved him fondly—more fondly than she believed she could ever love a mere cousin. But all that was passed and gone now, she thought with a sigh.

It was a hard and trying task to undertake, this enforced silence on a subject so near and dear to her heart; and it would prove, she knew, a sore test of fortitude throughout the day. Wherefore she embarked with a sorrowful heart, though determined to carry out to the letter her resolve to cross her cousin's path no more.

Too proud to let her emotions and her mental depression be observed—by Wilton in particular —she launched into the opposite extreme, giving free play to her brilliant conversational talents, feigning lightness of heart she was far, very far, from feeling.

What unwisdom in woman so to wear a mask and seek to deceive! Would she but see how her strength consists in her weakness, and how the most powerful weapon she can wield is an appeal to man's pity and sympathy, how much oftener would she hesitate to enter the dubious and dangerous paths of hypocrisy!—how much oftener would she open her heart and confide. her cares!—how much oftener would she speak the whole truth!—how much oftener shrink from flying into bitterness and hostility!

Alas for the folly and unreasoning frivolity of the human mind! That woman does ofttimes succeed by the use of deceptive arts is undeniable. But does she not likewise repeatedly miss the mark? Does she not repeatedly lose, instead of winning, affection by such vain devices? Then her wiles and schemes recoil on her own head, resulting in suspicion, distrust, and aversion.

Olinda concealed not her thoughts, nor did she act a part with the view of drawing back Henry to his allegiance by her assumed unconcern and gaiety of tone. Far from her were such unworthy intentions. Yet was she unwittingly practising deception, notwithstanding the scornful contempt in which she theoretically held the slightest departure from the truth. The deception, however, proceeded from no wrong motive. It was but the result of pardonable womanly pride—pride that would not let her stoop to betray and lay bare before Wilton's eyes how her heart was bleeding on his account.

Well did she enact her enforced part, engrossing the host all day long in earnest and animated conversation. She was by turns so "merry and wise" that she charmed by her quick bright ready wit, by her sparkling repartee, by her thoughtful disquisitions on many topics, by her large store of knowledge, and by her rare good sense. None suspected the sad secret. None read in her smiling animated countenance the efforts she made to be gay, nor the inward heartburnings she endured.

The marked footing of intimacy with which Olinda and Edwardes continued to converse, and the way in which they isolated themselves during the whole day from the rest, were duly noted by their companions, and regarded with considerable disfavour.

That her niece should monopolize one whom she hoped to have made her special property sorely irritated Miss Thornton, and made her profoundly jealous. On Wilton's account also she was angry with Olinda, for she firmly believed that her niece had already in Henry an engaged lover, to whom she was bound to devote all her attention.

As for Geraldine and Frederick, they were indignant at not being able to get hold of Edwardes and make him draw their silly aunt into a flirtation *au grand sérieux* for their special entertainment—a plot laid by Geraldine when the old lady praised Edwardes so warmly on the day of his introduction. Besides Geraldine noticed her brother's dejected air, and resented the vexation he felt, as it appeared to her, through the cruel and unseemly neglect of Olinda.

Henry himself got the absurd belief into his head that Olinda was already captivated by their good-looking host, and he silently deplored her degeneracy in offering such a sacrifice on the altar of talent as to devote herself in such a marked way to a man several years her senior, and who, despite his learning and mental endowments, was decidedly her inferior in refinement.

He now longed to be her mentor, as she had previously striven to be his. Wilton well knew that Edwardes entertained no designs on Olinda, but feared that he possessed sufficient attractions to win, albeit unintentionally, the unsophisticated though clever and brilliant girl. If the prospect of his lot united to Azzahra appeared deplorable in Olinda's sight, how far worse should she consider her own—the wife of a pedant!

He chose to set down Edwardes as a pedant because he loved discoursing on learned themes. But he overlooked the fact that his friend knew how to comport himself as a perfect gentleman, and that, as a rule, he only indulged in discussions on dry subjects among scientific companions, or among those who he thought would make allowances for his long-acquired habits, and would appreciate such conversation.

Henry forgot, too, that Olinda's inconsiderate devotion to talent was for the gift more than for its possessor. He forgot that, though she might be carried away at times with unreasoning avidity by a fair-spoken aspirant for distinction and fame who set himself up above his fellows, her infatuation was but fleeting and momentary. He forgot that the abilities and mental acquirements of a man devoted to the pursuits of literature may be blindly worshipped by a woman, although his personal qualifications may never have attracted her attention—still less, gained her affection.

And this was the footing on which Olinda cultivated the society of Edwardes. She looked with reverent respect on his scientific excellence, his social attainments, and his marked strength of character, but never for a moment did she regard him in the light of a lover. Such an idea she would have scouted as preposterous. The man to whom she would surrender her liberty must be of a far higher grade. He must outshine all rivals, herself even, by the lustre of his genius and wit. He must border closely on having all the attributes of perfection. Such an one alone could she look up to and love—such an one alone could she allow to rule over her !

Absurd egotistical folly ! Where could such a paragon of perfection be met with ?

To this height of mental qualification Edwardes assuredly did not and could not attain. With wisdom, knowledge, and ability he was abundantly endowed, though, to some extent, he undoubtedly lacked polish and refinement such as can captivate the female heart. He was material, not spiritual. He was mind, not soul. He was of the earth, earthy.

As such, though too harshly, Olinda summed him up, striving in her folly after unattainable perfection.

But Wilton suspected not that she regarded Edwardes in this light, for he judged by sight. So far as he could discern, she had purposely and studiously made herself conspicuous with this man, almost a stranger, in a way that had filled him with constant pain. Though his heart no longer yearned for his cousin, he was deeply offended that she had so slighted him, and that their new acquaintance should have been thus preferred before him.

They were sailing past the fort at the mouth of the Oued Khremis, a small river flowing down from the Lesser Atlas Mountains through the Metidja, when a sudden sharp concussion, that shook the Atlanta from stem to stern, spread consternation on deck. The yacht had grounded on a sandbank opposite the river's mouth, and, giving a heavy lurch, she heeled over slightly to leeward.

A universal demolition of glass and crockery ensued, which was being laid out in the cabin for luncheon by Edwardes's valet and the steward of the Atlanta. Tables and chairs followed the example, creating a deafening clatter, accompanied by the loud flapping of sails, the clashing of spars and yards, and the shouts of the crew in their efforts to right the vessel—a bewildering chaos of sound, which filled the ladies of the party with dismay.

Edwardes lost no time, after taking in the sails, in launching and manning the boats, and the artillery soldiers quartered in the fort close by rowed out to their assistance. But all efforts to get off the cutter proved ineffectual. She remained fixed and immovable, firmly imbedded in the soft sand washed down from the mountains by the winter floods. The wind being light, and the yacht resting on clear smooth ground, Edwardes saw there was no further cause for uneasiness, as no danger from the wind rising could be looked for before the arrival of assistance from Algiers.

"I hope she will be none the worse for this," Edwardes exclaimed, as he surveyed the stranded vessel, "for I expect great things from her next season at Cowes."

His guests, as bound in politeness, freely added their good wishes, and expressed their hope that the Atlanta might be safely floated off before any unfavourable change in the weather should take place.

By this time they had recovered their equanimity, with the exception of Miss Thornton, and awaited the course of events with patient complacency. The simulated alarm of that venerable spinster at the untoward catastrophe was unbounded, and she caused general merriment by her frantic gesticulations and exclamations of terror. With helplessness almost infantine she attached herself to Edwardes, clinging wildly to him in her distress as to a saving protector—a palpable stroke of barefaced coquetry highly entertaining to Geraldine and Frederick. In vain she was assured that not the smallest danger existed, as the vessel could not possibly be injured by the gentle breeze that was blowing. But she would not be comforted, continuing to moan aloud with vigorous pertinacity.

Seeing her distress, Wilton roused himself from the gloomy reverie in which he had long been absorbed, and hastened to her assistance— an act of kindness by no means appreciated, for she seemed grievously disappointed that their host had not volunteered to offer his condolence.

The boats soon took the party off, depositing them in safety on the sandy shore beneath the old city of Rusgunia. Not a vestige of a harbour nor even of a landing-place was visible, so the sailors ran the boats on to the smooth beach, dragging them up afterwards, as had doubtless been done by the ancient inhabitants of the town many hundreds of years before.

After weary waiting on the cliffs, the party gladly beheld the tug, for which a horseman had been dispatched by land, get up steam and bear down towards them from the distant harbour of Algiers. She was not long in running across the bay and drawing up alongside the helpless Atlanta. A hawser was made fast to the yacht, and after a few hearty heaves she was floating once more in deep water, sound and buoyant as ever.

As soon as she was free all joyfully hastened down to the beach, and jumped into the boats to return on board, except Alice Thornton, who stoutly declared she would rather walk the whole way round than brave again the perils of the deep. But finding that none volunteered to be her escort in this feat of pedestrianism, reflecting moreover that the distance was great and the day was now far spent, she allowed her scruples to be overcome, and silently embarked with her companions.

After a rapid run in tow of the steamer, the Atlanta entered the harbour and swung round once more at her moorings, in no respect the worse for her unfortunate misadventure. When the excitement of the mishap they met with subsided, Wilton relapsed into his melancholy reflections about Olinda. He resolved to take an early opportunity of telling her with what pain he had witnessed her remarkable behaviour with Edwardes, in the hope of checking such folly and heedless want of forethought.

Little he suspected that one more dangerous far than Edwardes was at hand, who was to bring in his train ruin, havoc, and despair!

END OF VOL. I.

PRINTED BY VIRTUE AND CO., LIMITED, CITY ROAD, LONDON.

Lightning Source UK Ltd.
Milton Keynes UK
UKHW020141191118
332579UK00007B/117/P